D0538499

THIS BOOK IS DEDICATED TO PELE, AUGUST AND EPPIE, THE AUTHOR'S THREE WONDERFUL CATS.

Copyright ©2010 Aron Nels Steinke.
Balloon Toons™ is a registered
trademark of Harriet Ziefert, Inc.
All rights reserved/CIP data is available.
Published in the United Sates 2010 by
Blue Apple Books,
515 Valley Street, Maplewood, NJ 07040
www.blueapplebooks.com

Distributed in the U.S. by Chronicle Books
First Edition
Printed in China 09/10
ISBN: 978-1-60905-035-1

2 4 6 8 10 9 7 5 3 1

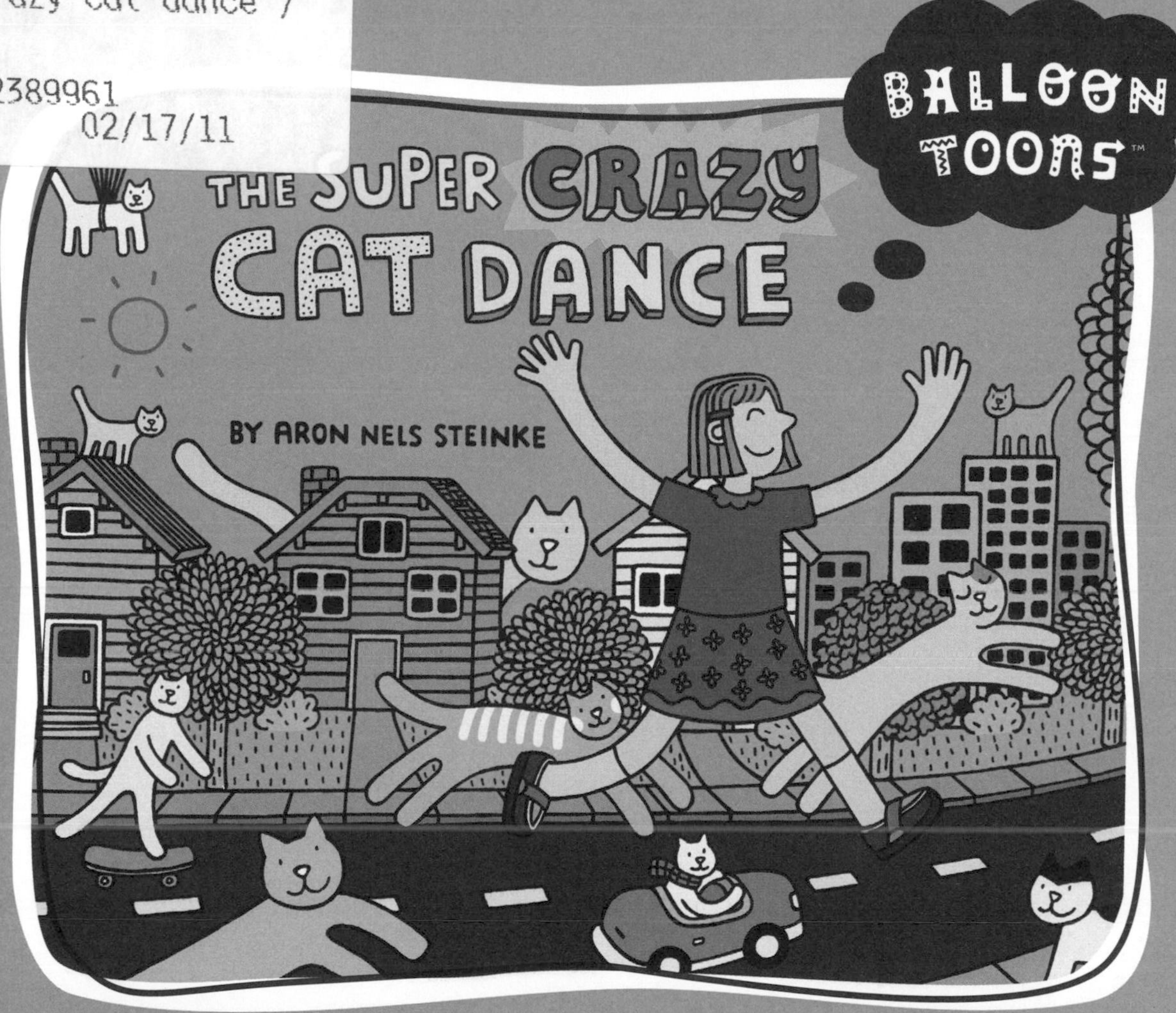
BALLOON TOONS™
THE SUPER CRAZY CAT DANCE
BY ARON NELS STEINKE

BLUE APPLE BOOKS

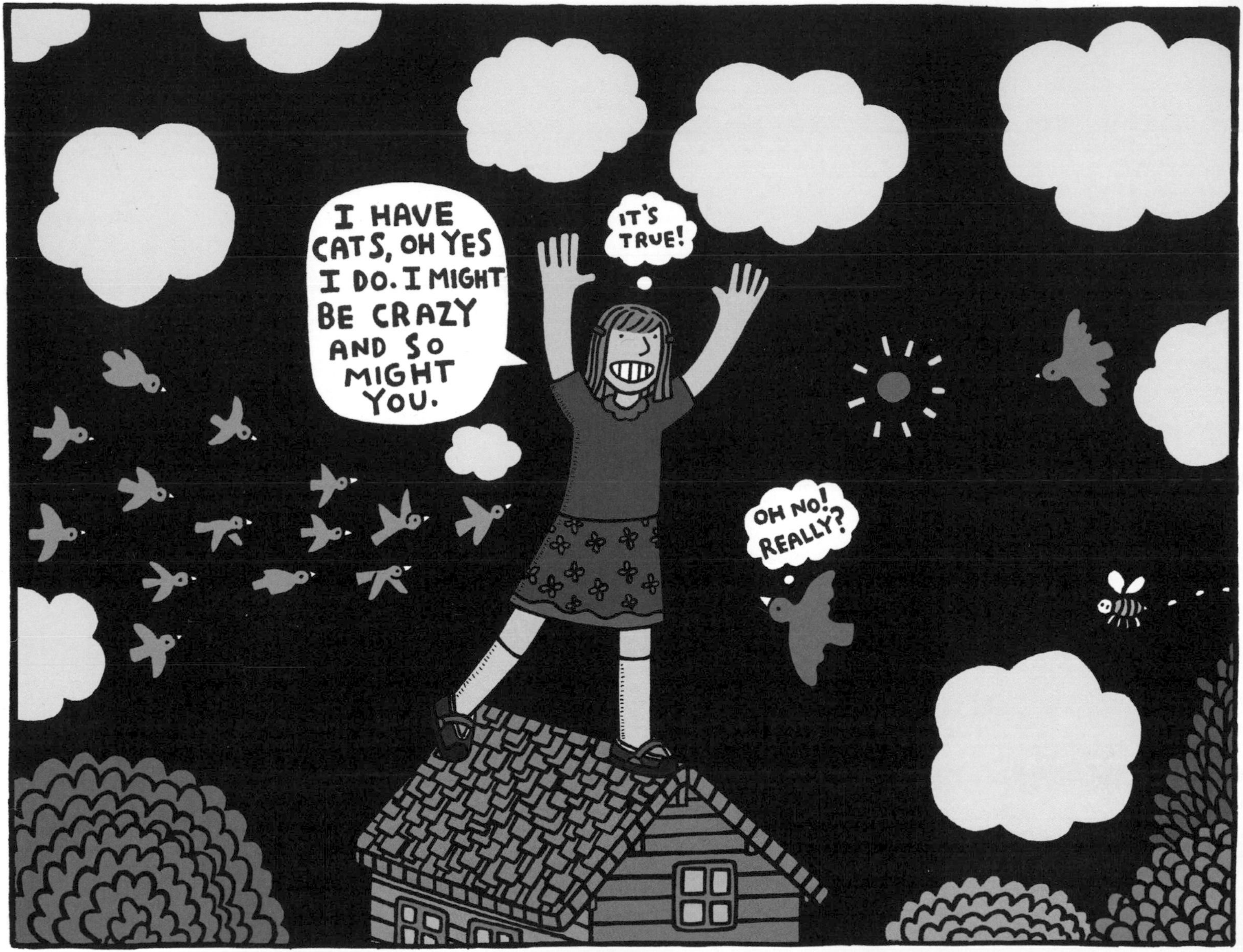
I HAVE CATS, OH YES I DO. I MIGHT BE CRAZY AND SO MIGHT YOU.
IT'S TRUE!
OH NO! REALLY?

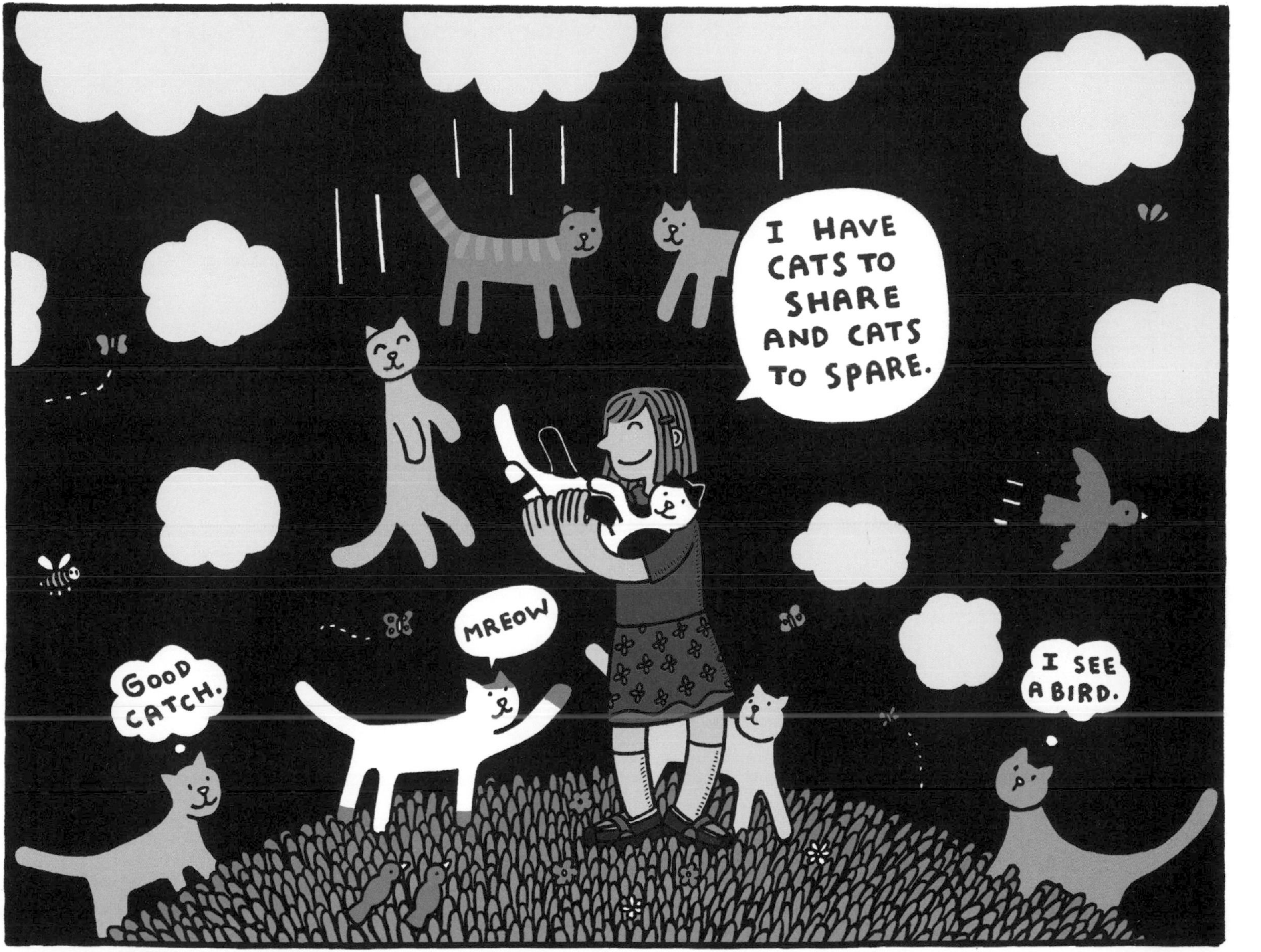
I HAVE CATS TO SHARE AND CATS TO SPARE.
MREOW
GOOD CATCH.
I SEE A BIRD.

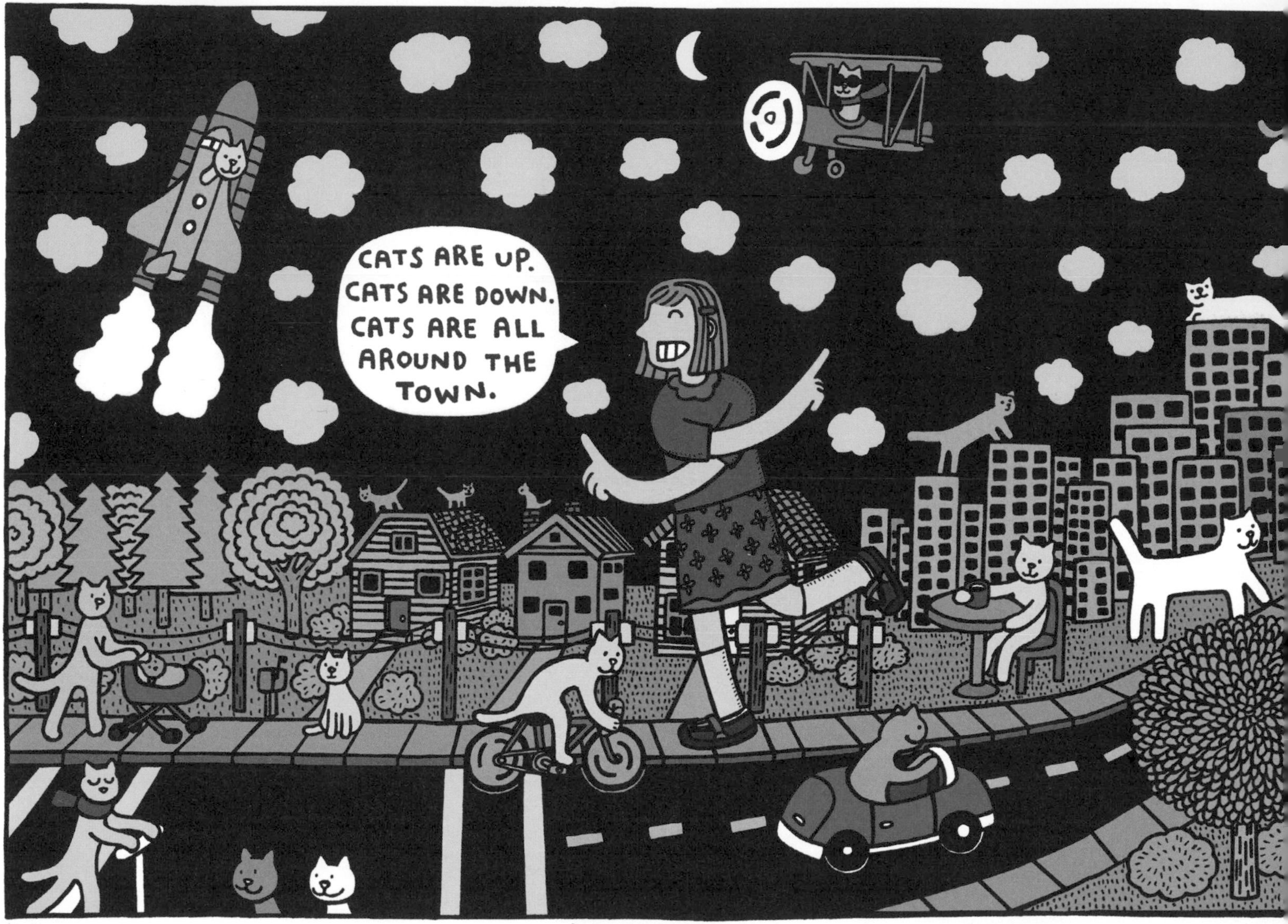
CATS ARE UP.
CATS ARE DOWN.
CATS ARE ALL
AROUND THE
TOWN.

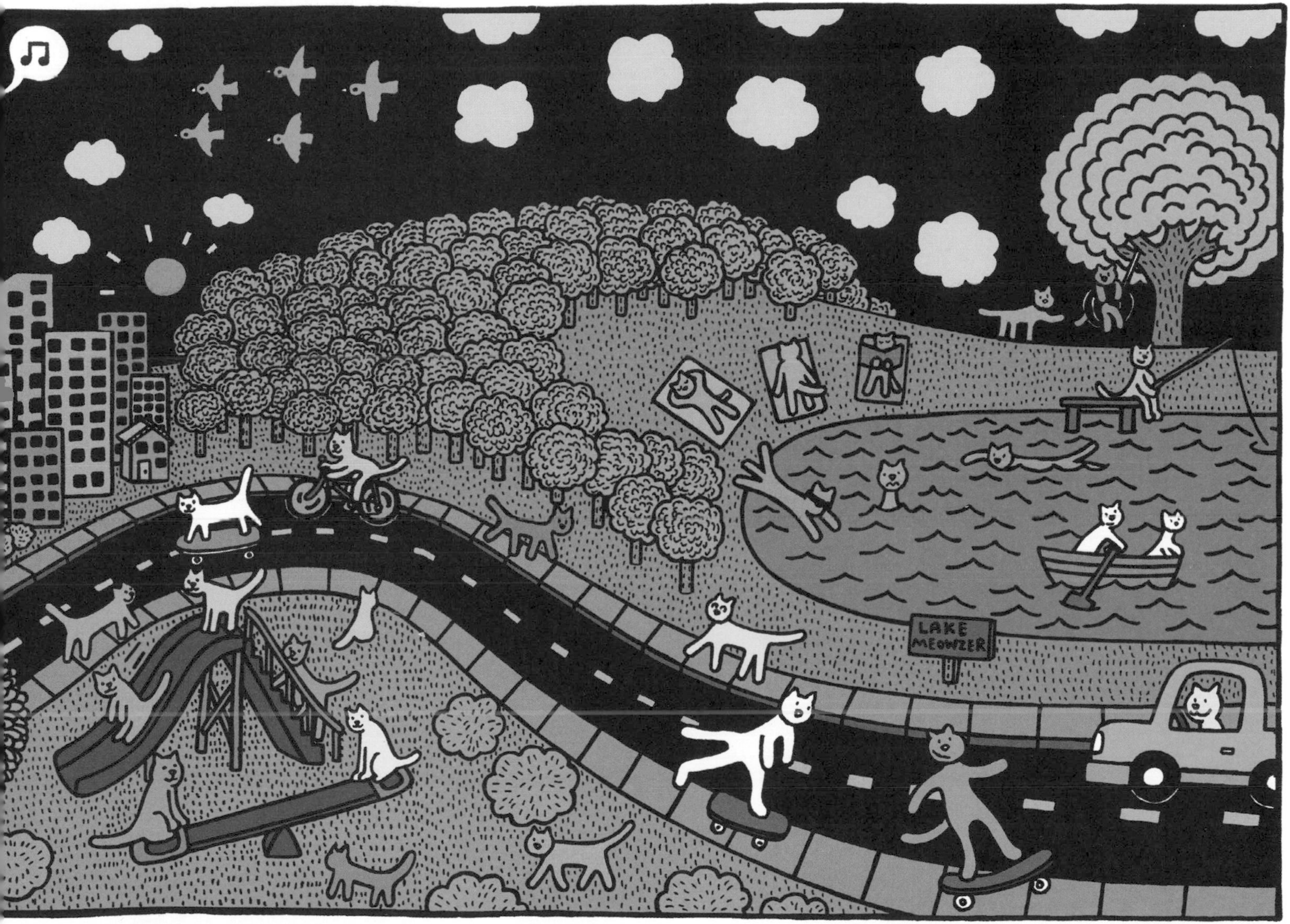
LAKE
MEOWZER

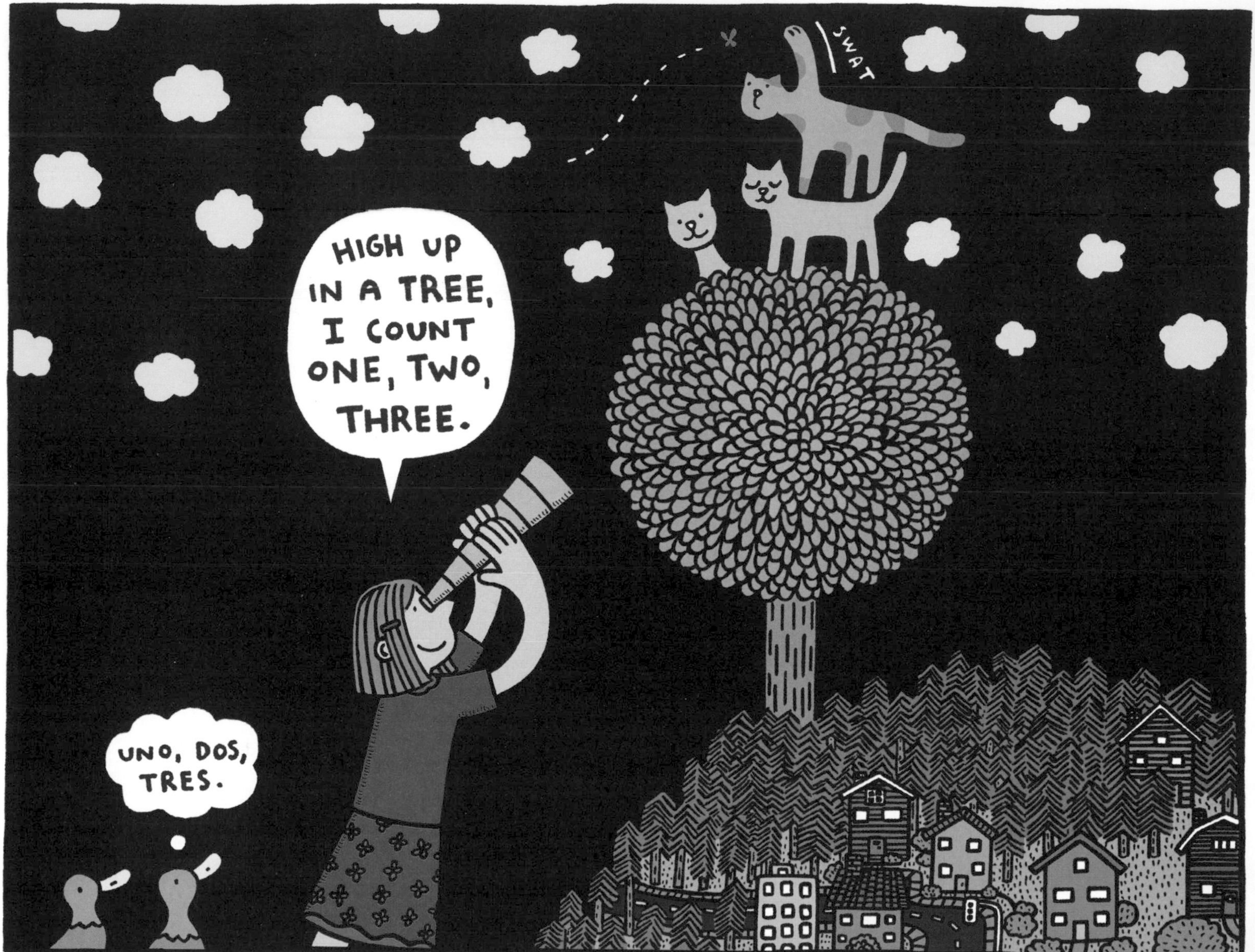
SWAT
HIGH UP IN A TREE, I COUNT ONE, TWO, THREE.
UNO, DOS, TRES.

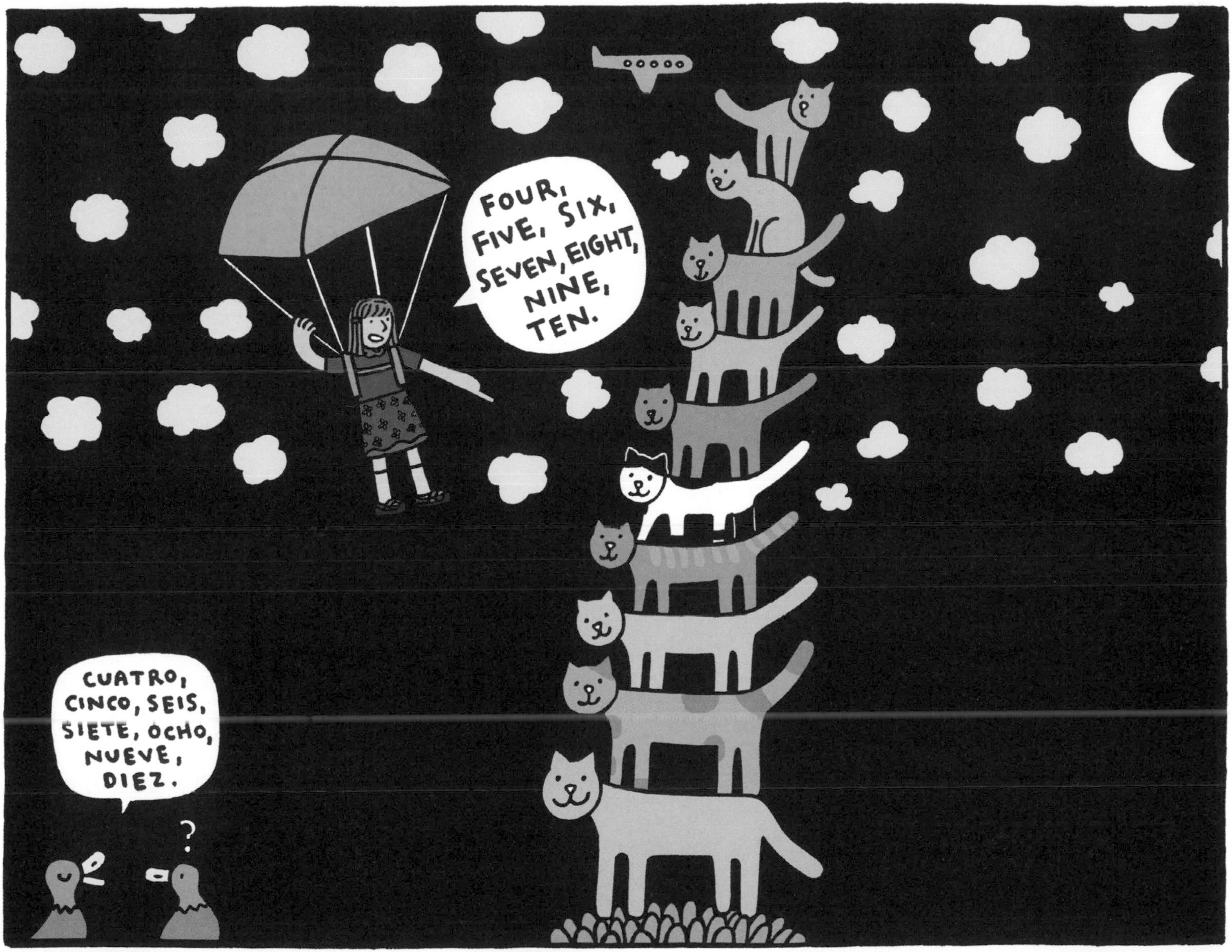
FOUR, FIVE, SIX, SEVEN, EIGHT, NINE, TEN.
CUATRO, CINCO, SEIS, SIETE, OCHO, NUEVE, DIEZ.
?

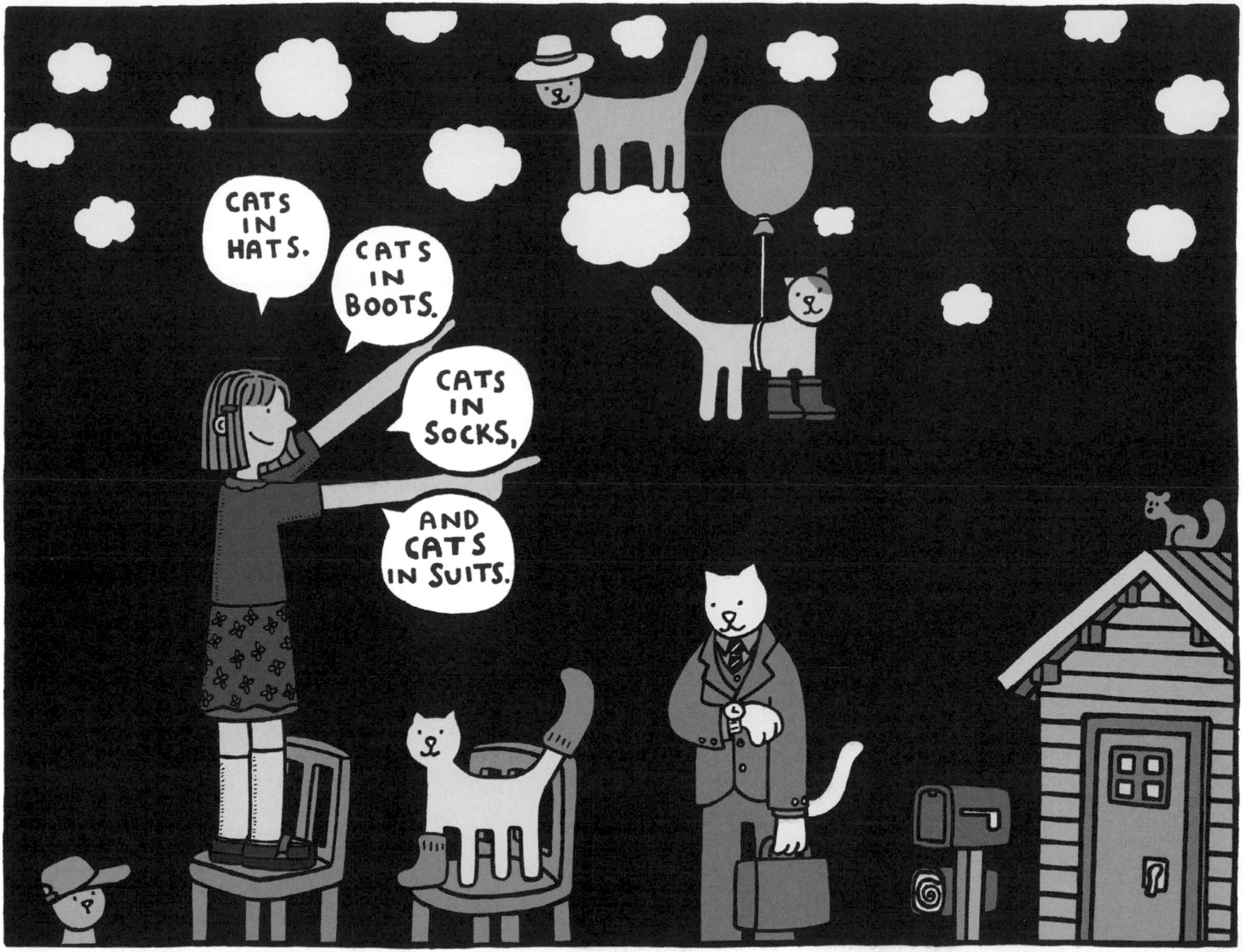
CATS IN HATS.
CATS IN BOOTS.
CATS IN SOCKS,
AND CATS IN SUITS.

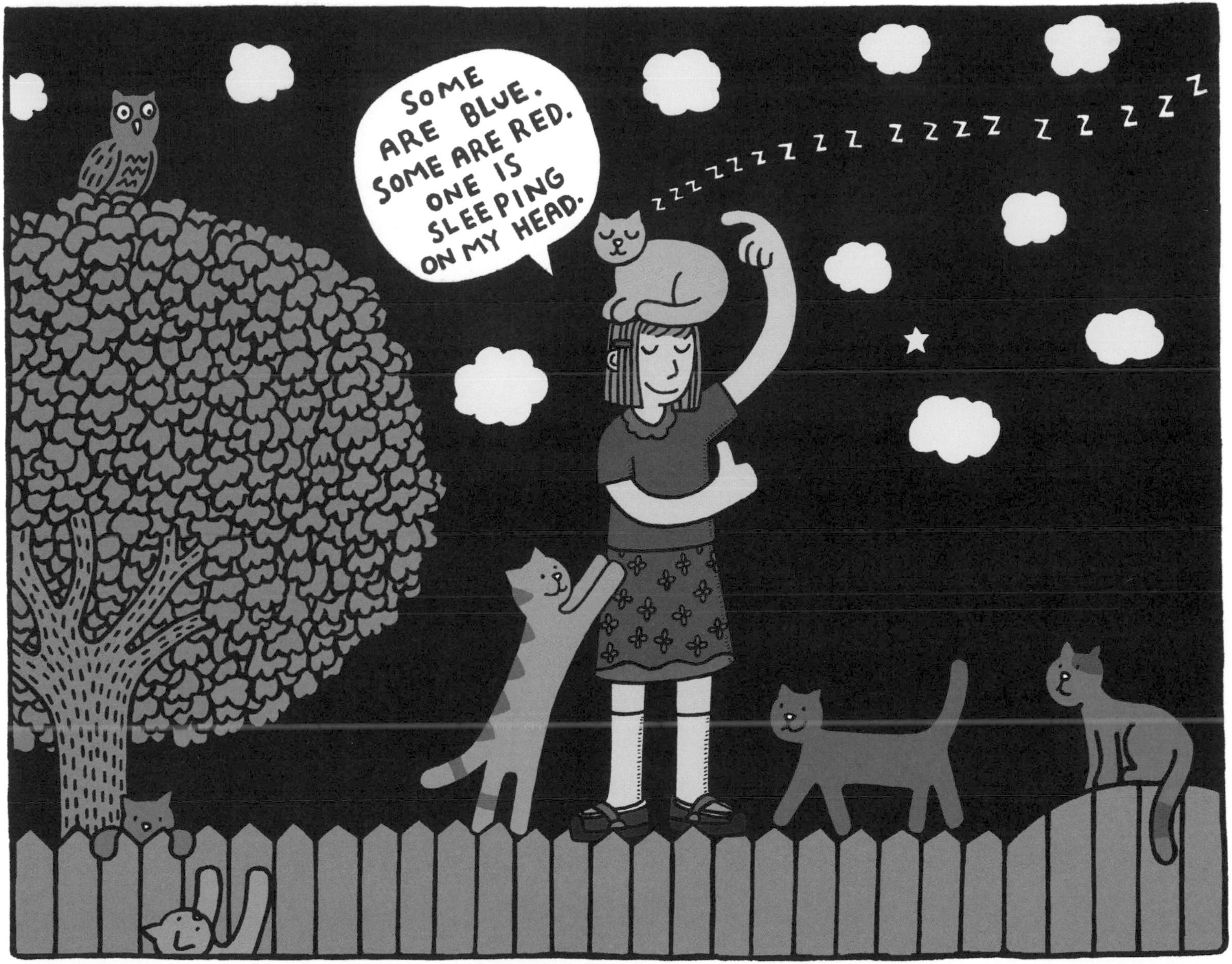
SOME ARE BLUE. SOME ARE RED. ONE IS SLEEPING ON MY HEAD.
Z Z Z Z Z Z Z Z Z Z Z Z Z Z Z Z Z Z Z Z Z Z

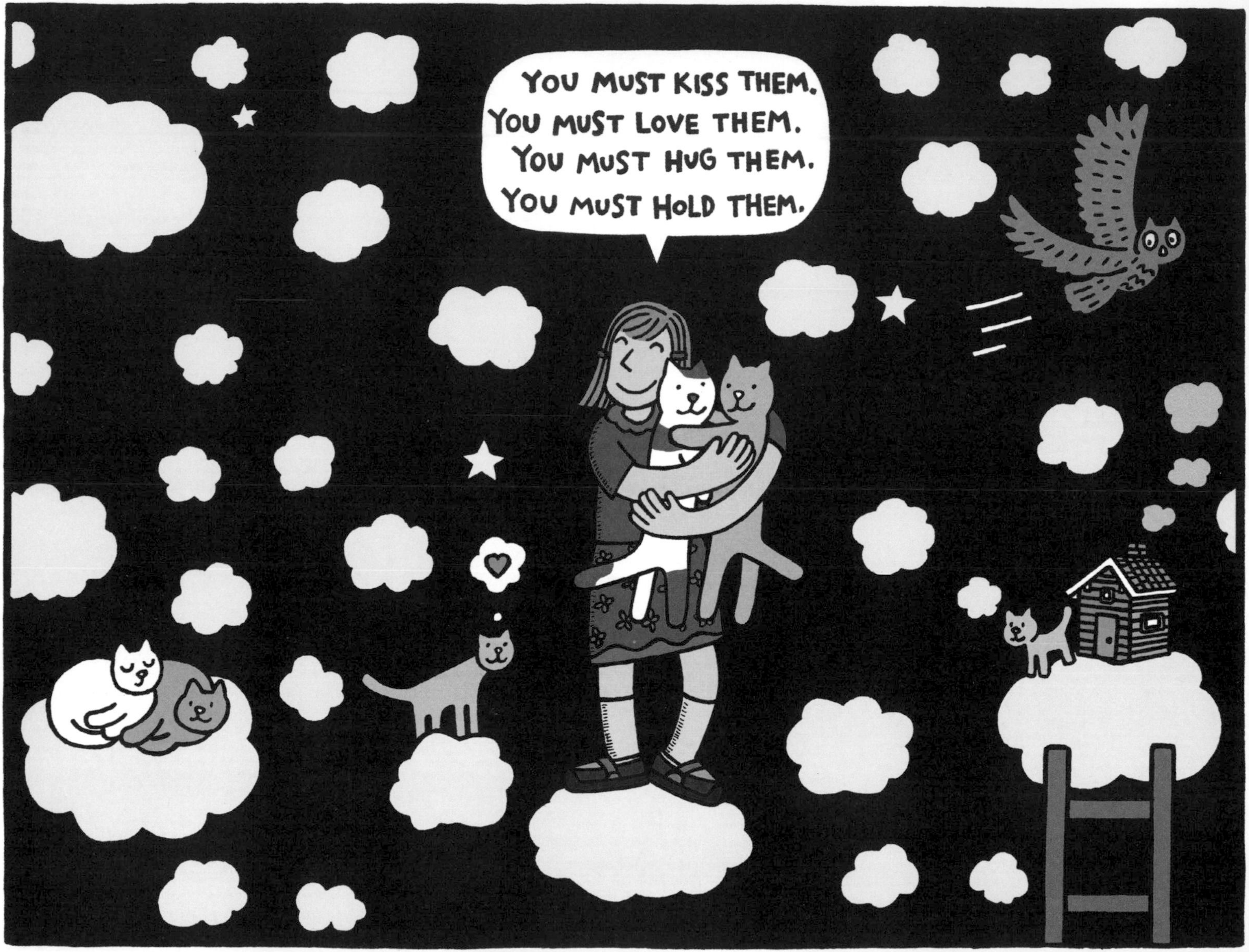
YOU MUST KISS THEM.
YOU MUST LOVE THEM.
YOU MUST HUG THEM.
YOU MUST HOLD THEM.

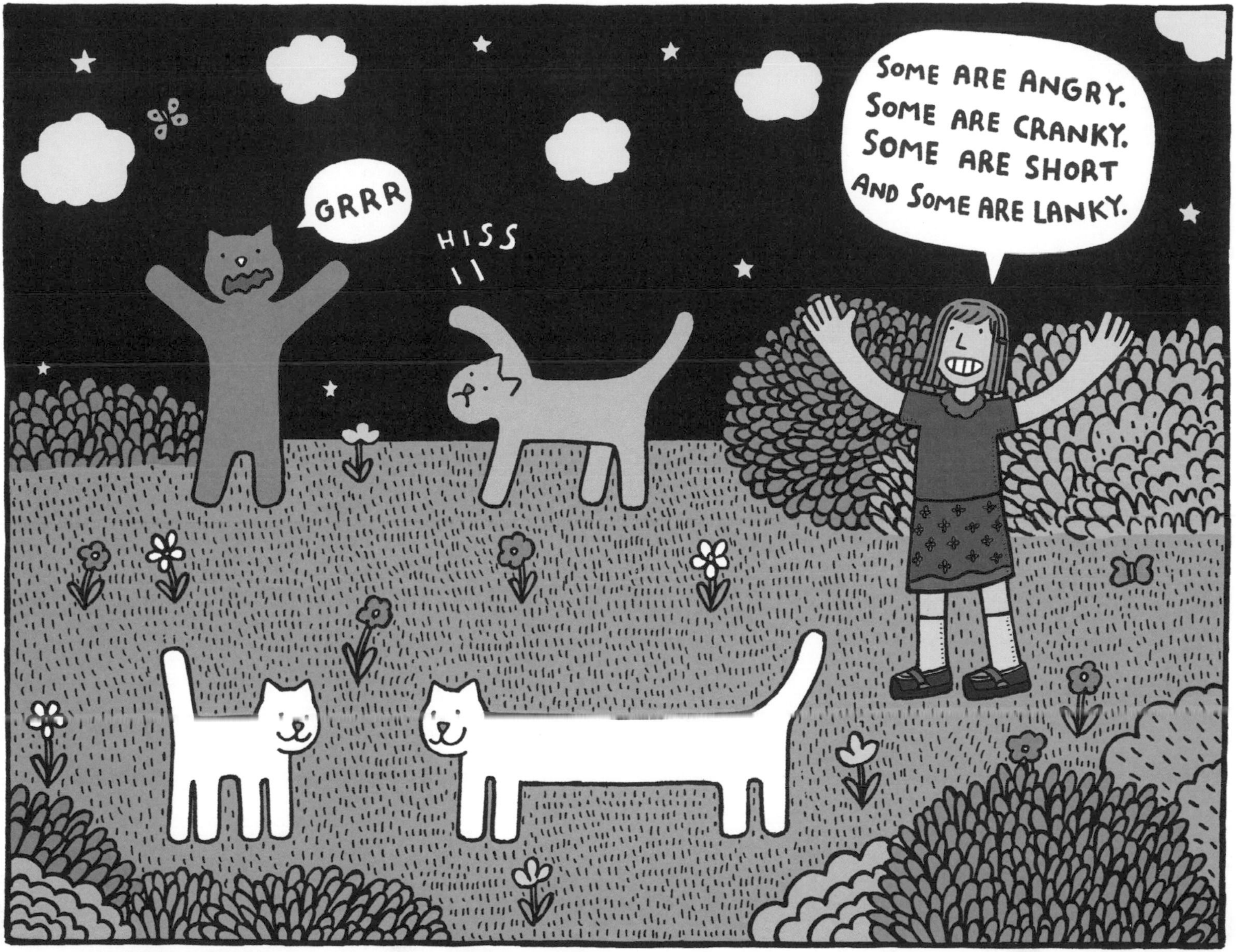
GRRR
HISS
SOME ARE ANGRY. SOME ARE CRANKY. SOME ARE SHORT AND SOME ARE LANKY.

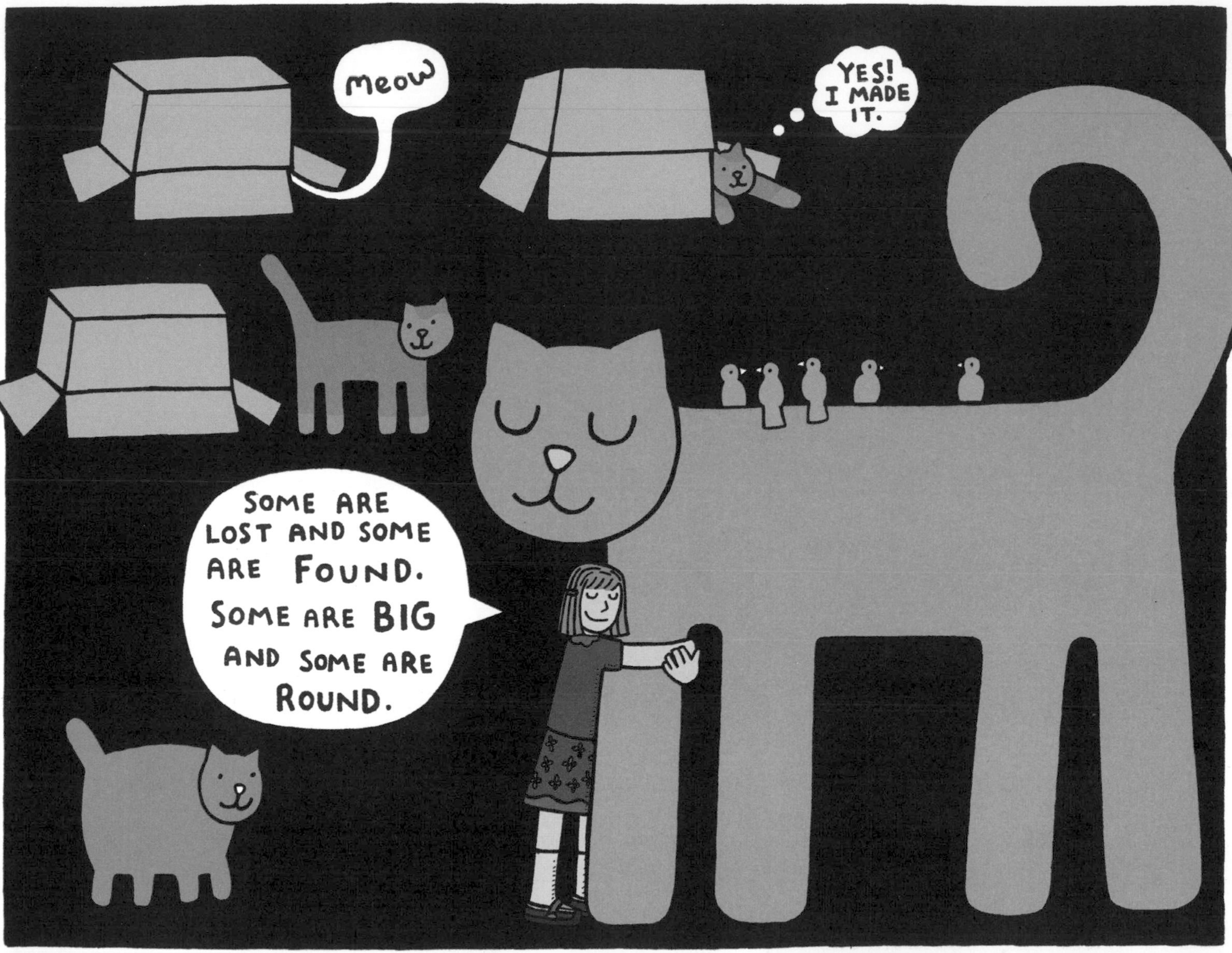
meow
YES! I MADE IT.
SOME ARE LOST AND SOME ARE FOUND. SOME ARE BIG AND SOME ARE ROUND.

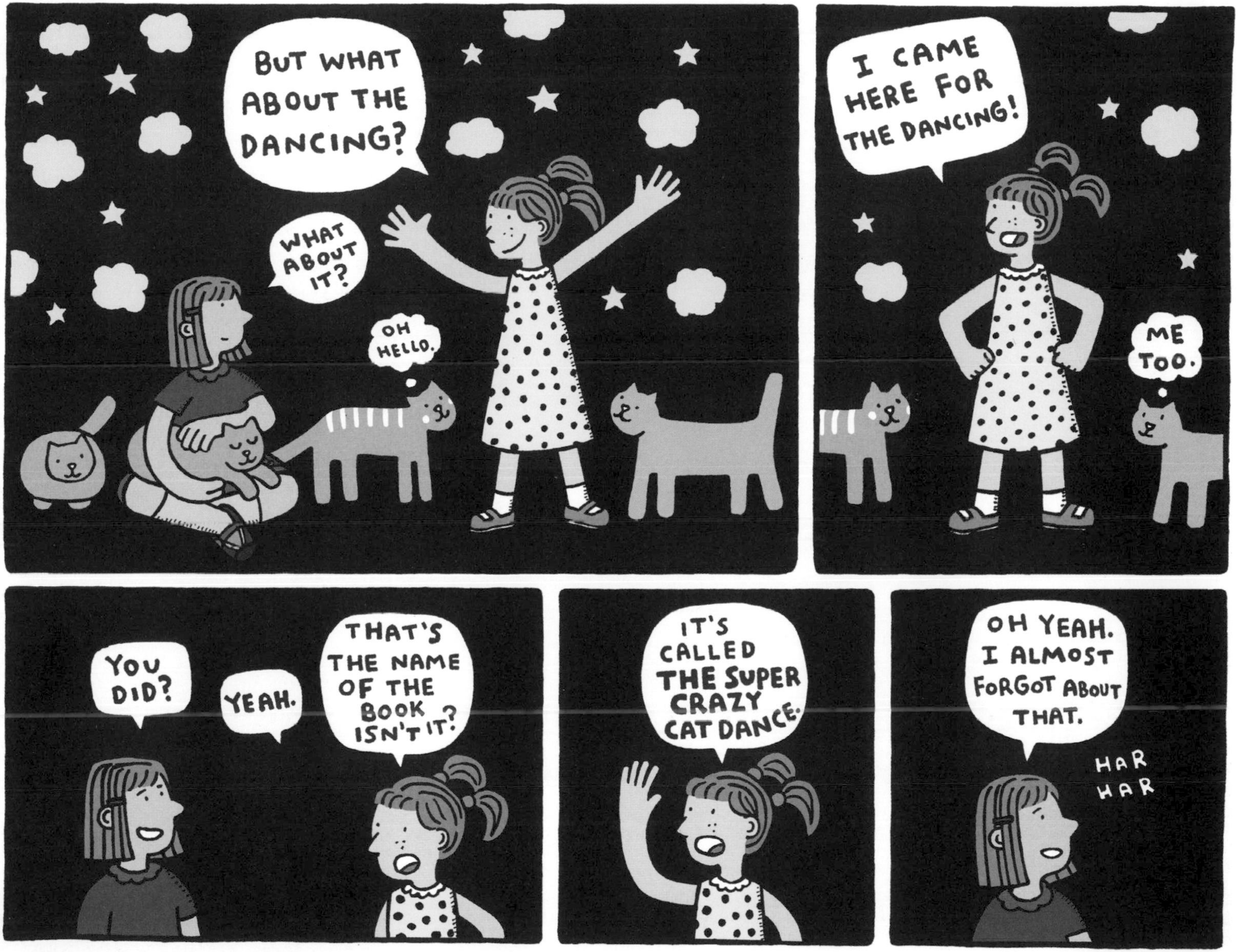
BUT WHAT ABOUT THE DANCING?
WHAT ABOUT IT?
OH HELLO.
I CAME HERE FOR THE DANCING!
ME TOO.
YOU DID?
YEAH.
THAT'S THE NAME OF THE BOOK ISN'T IT?
IT'S CALLED THE SUPER CRAZY CAT DANCE.
OH YEAH. I ALMOST FORGOT ABOUT THAT.
HAR HAR

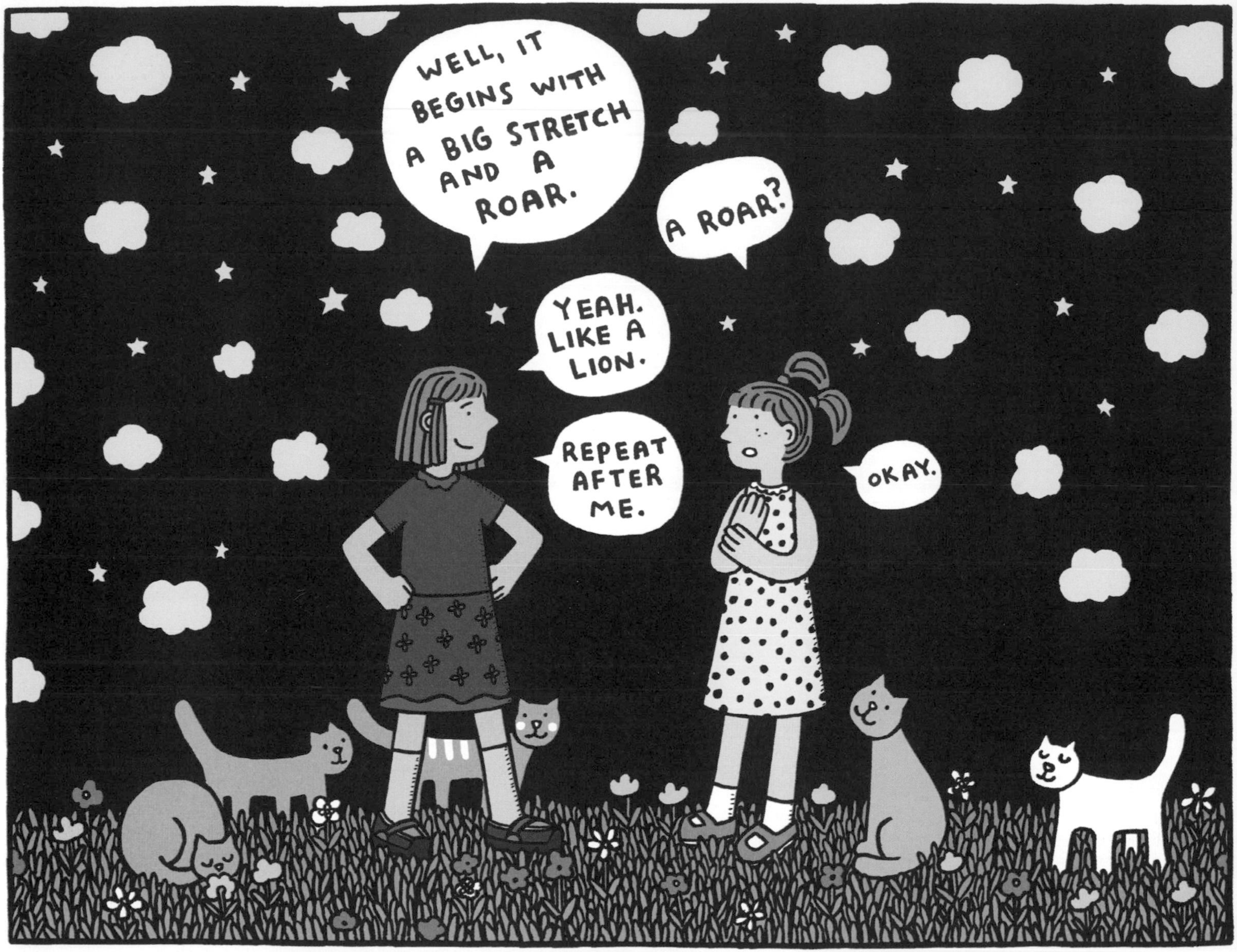
WELL, IT BEGINS WITH A BIG STRETCH AND A ROAR.
A ROAR?
YEAH. LIKE A LION.
REPEAT AFTER ME.
OKAY.

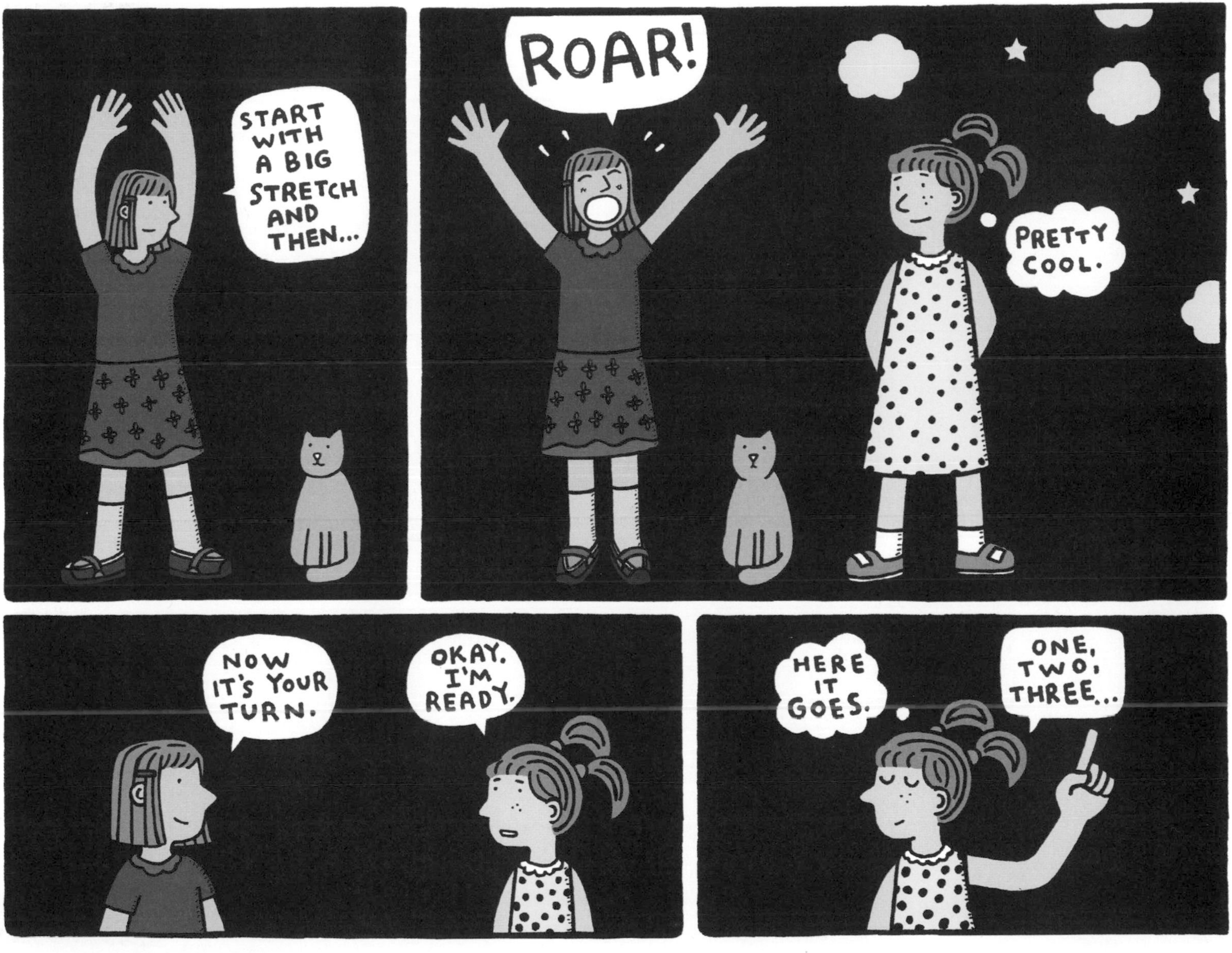
START WITH A BIG STRETCH AND THEN...
ROAR!
PRETTY COOL.
NOW IT'S YOUR TURN.
OKAY. I'M READY.
HERE IT GOES.
ONE, TWO, THREE...

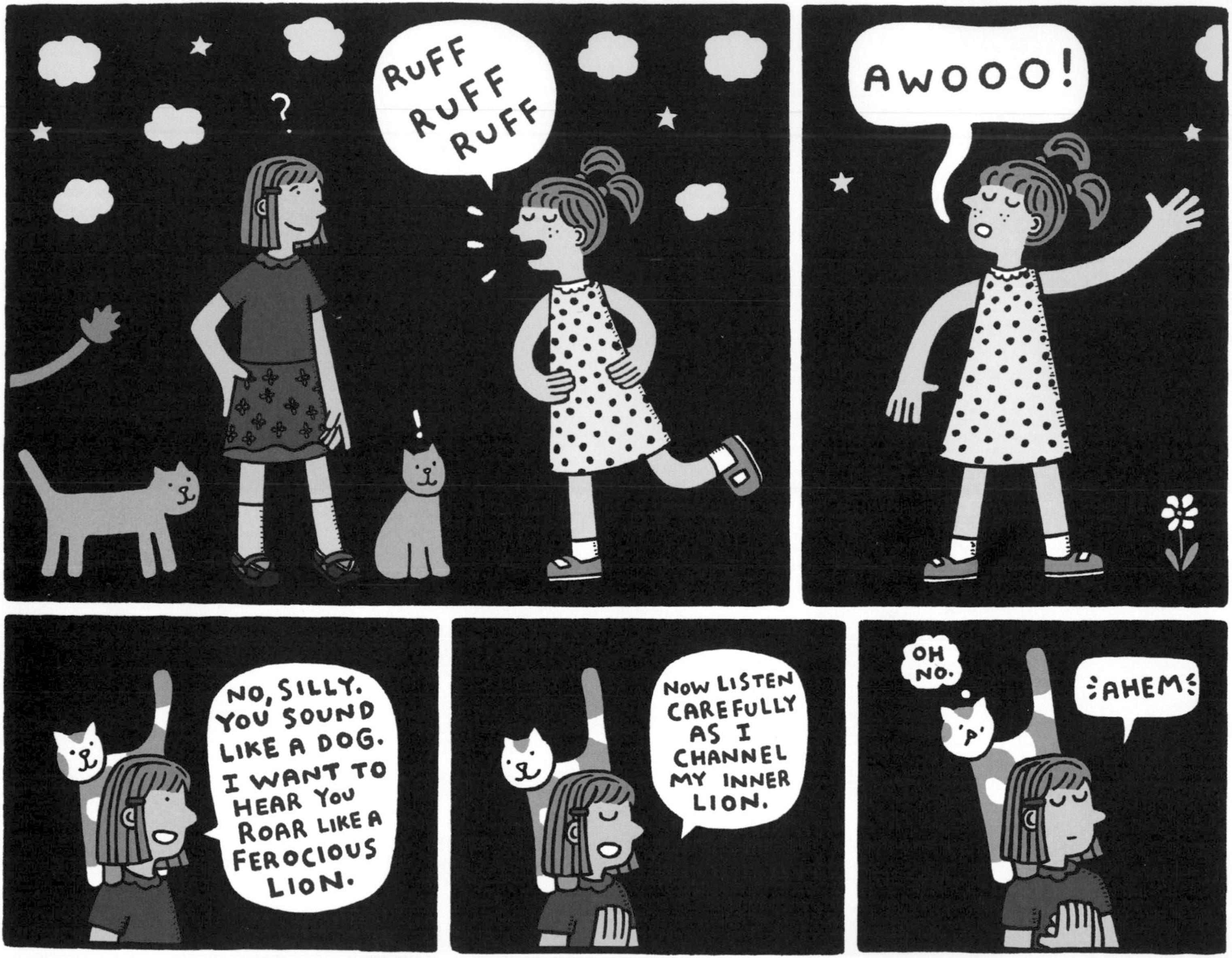
?
RUFF RUFF RUFF
!
AWOOO!
NO, SILLY. YOU SOUND LIKE A DOG. I WANT TO HEAR YOU ROAR LIKE A FEROCIOUS LION.
NOW LISTEN CAREFULLY AS I CHANNEL MY INNER LION.
OH NO.
AHEM

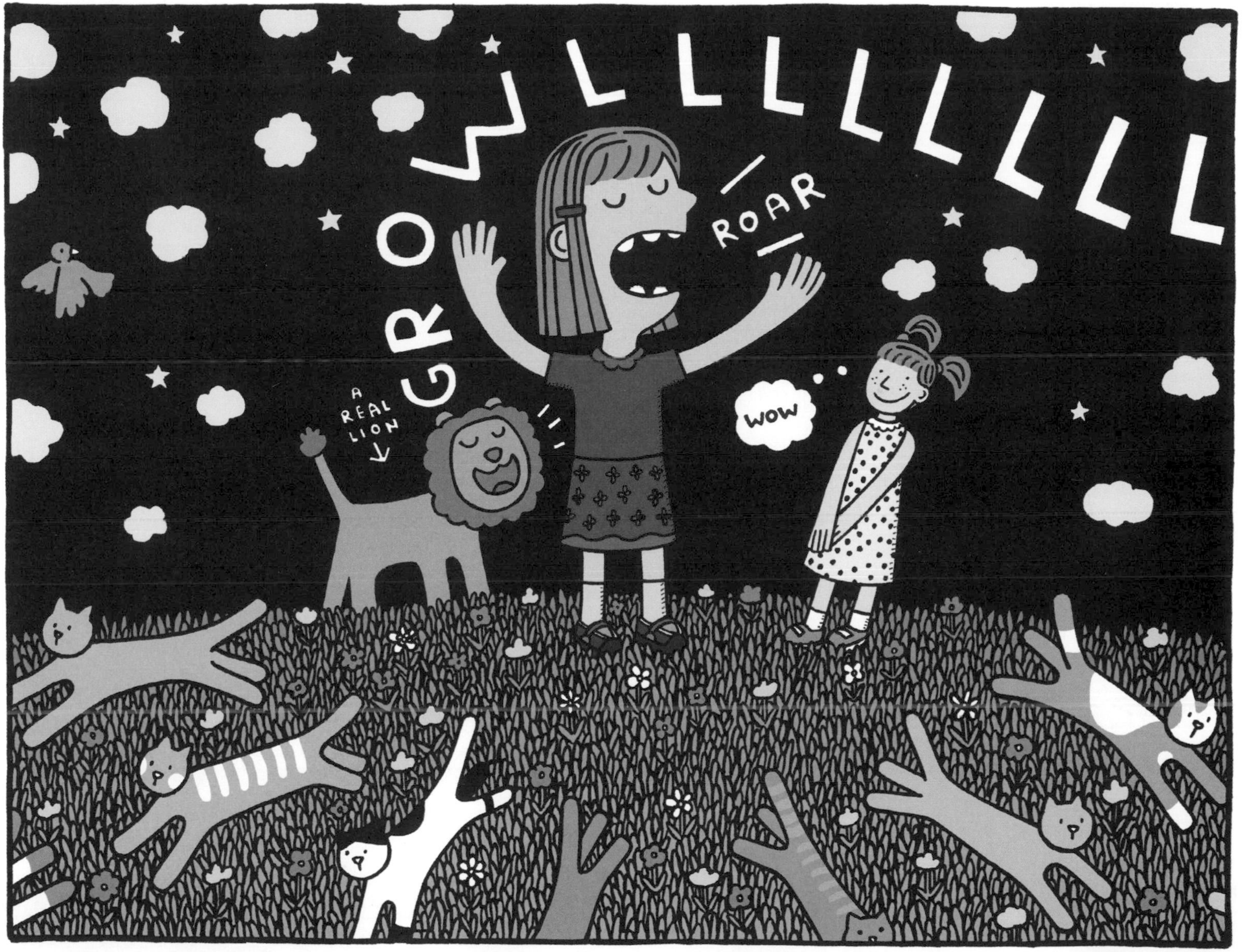
GROWLLLLLLLLLL
ROAR
A REAL LION
WOW

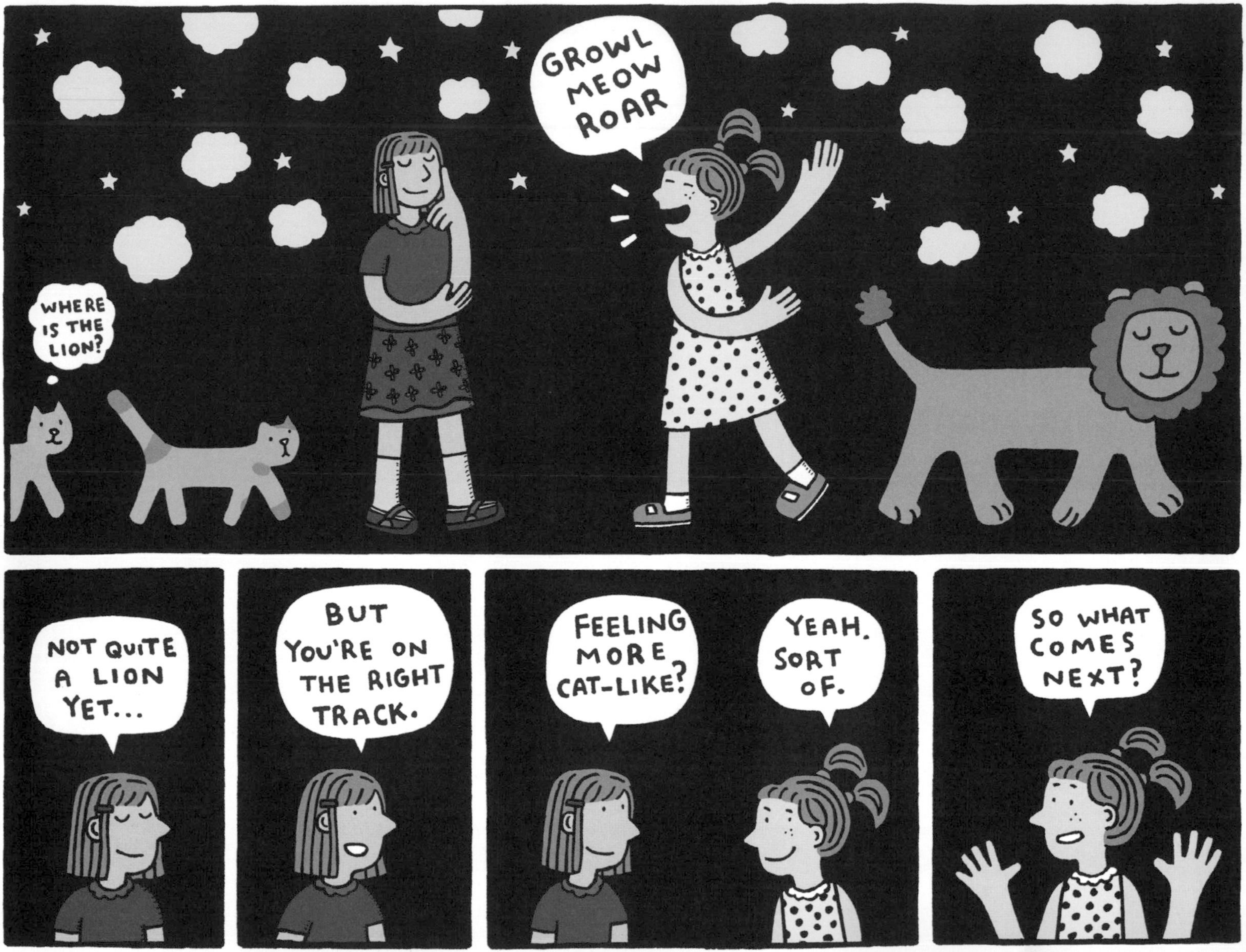
WHERE IS THE LION?
GROWL MEOW ROAR
NOT QUITE A LION YET...
BUT YOU'RE ON THE RIGHT TRACK.
FEELING MORE CAT-LIKE?
YEAH. SORT OF.
SO WHAT COMES NEXT?

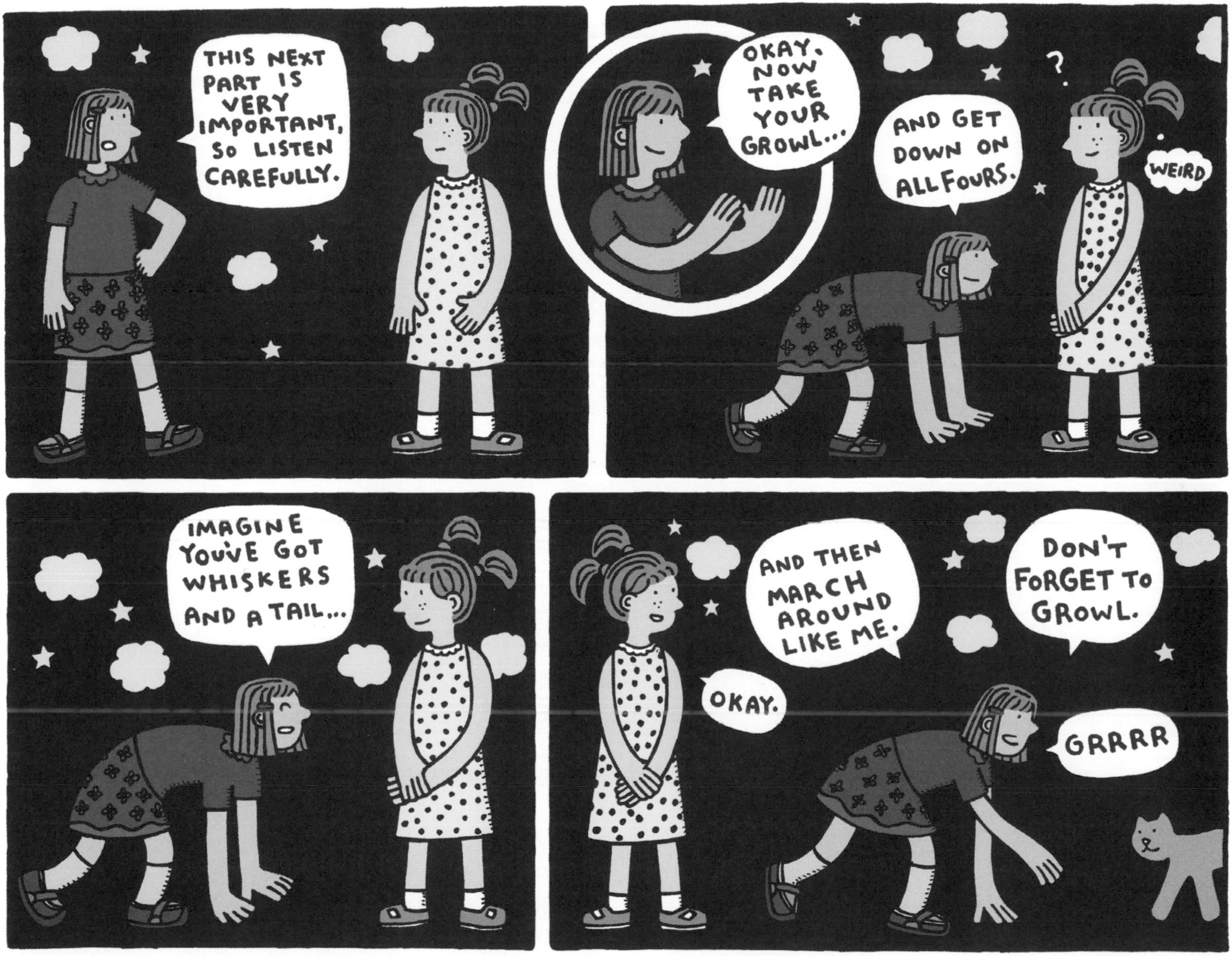
THIS NEXT PART IS VERY IMPORTANT, SO LISTEN CAREFULLY.
OKAY. NOW TAKE YOUR GROWL...
AND GET DOWN ON ALL FOURS.
?
WEIRD
IMAGINE YOU'VE GOT WHISKERS AND A TAIL...
AND THEN MARCH AROUND LIKE ME.
DON'T FORGET TO GROWL.
OKAY.
GRRRR

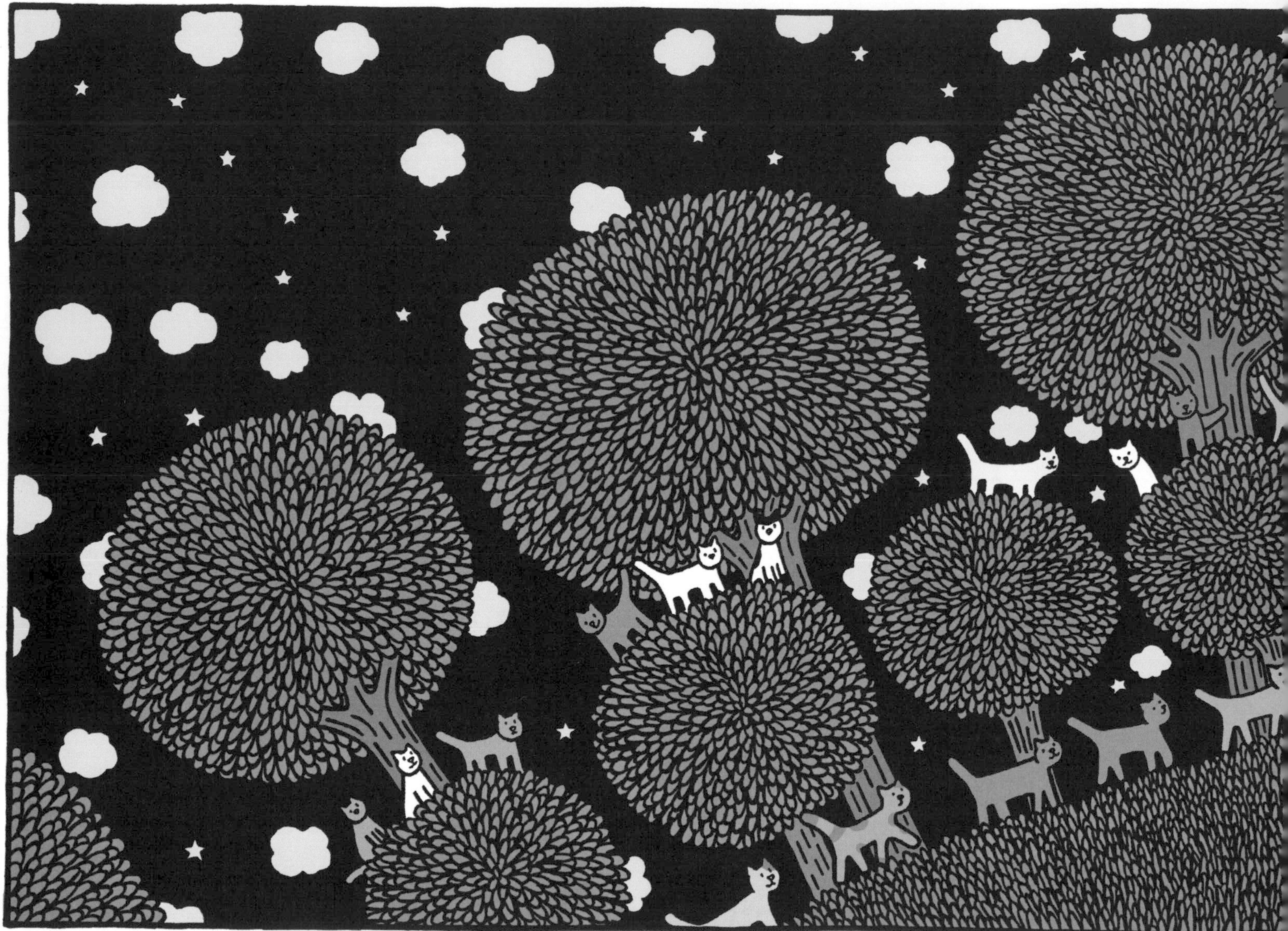

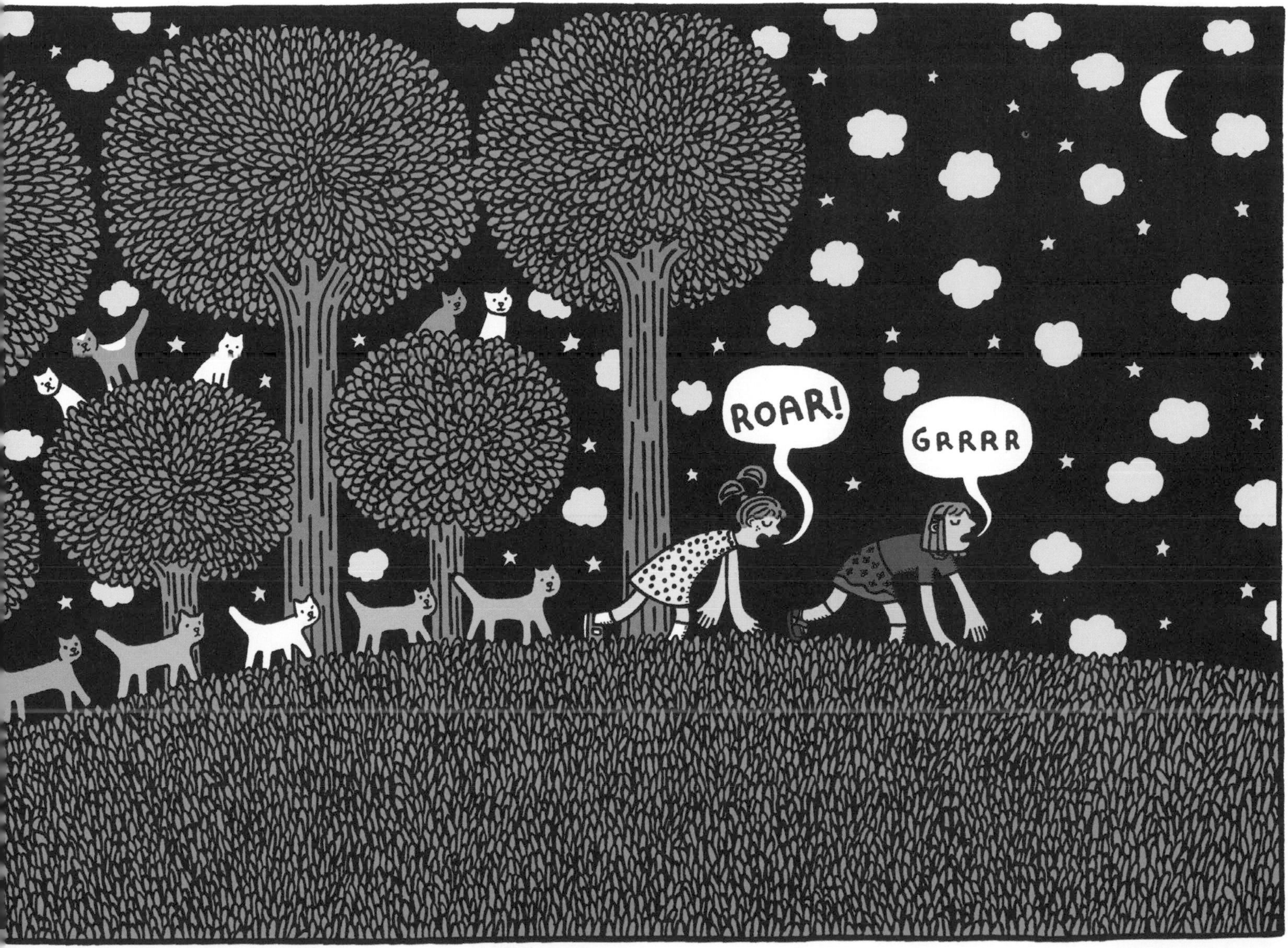
ROAR!
GRRRR

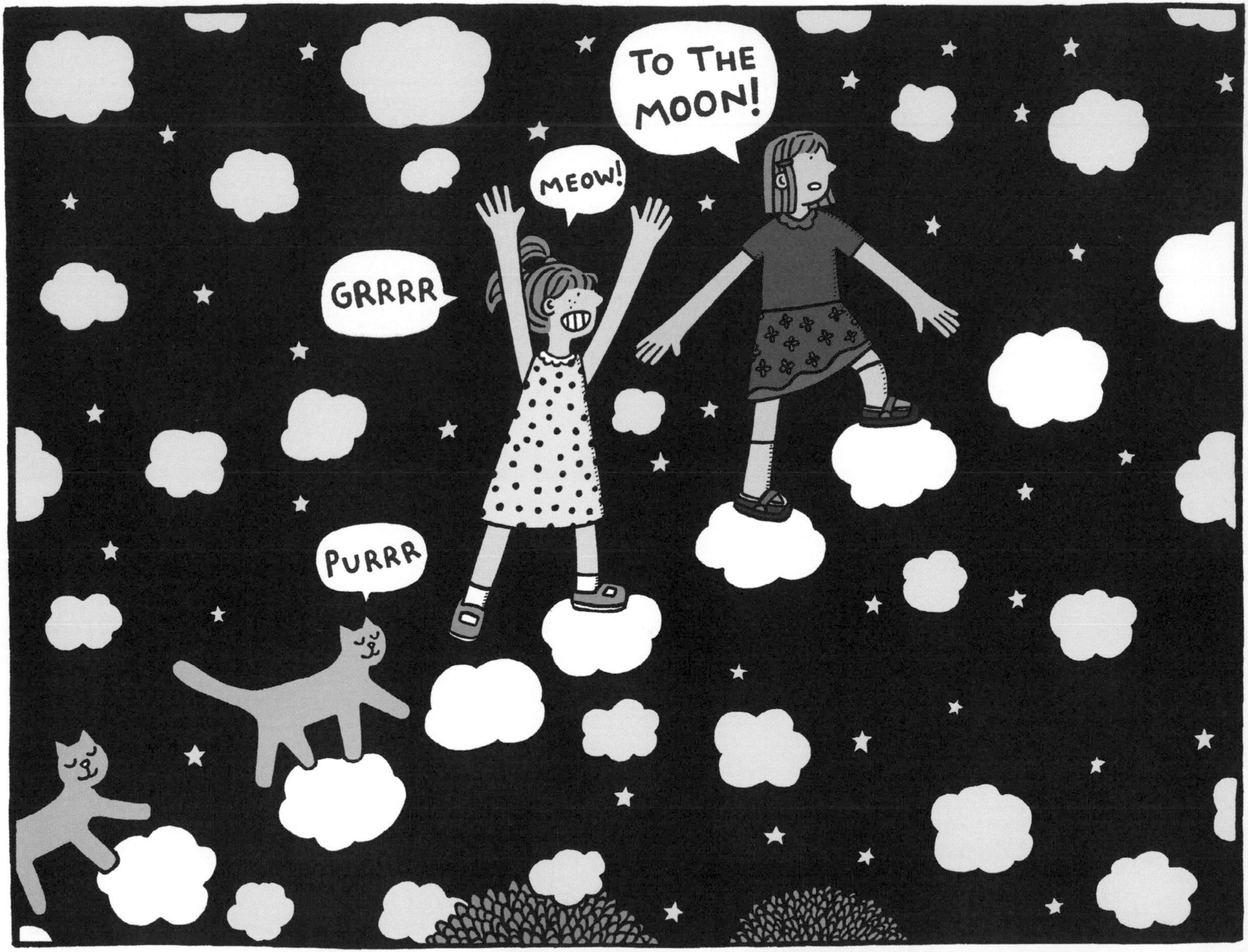
TO THE MOON!
MEOW!
GRRRR
PURRR

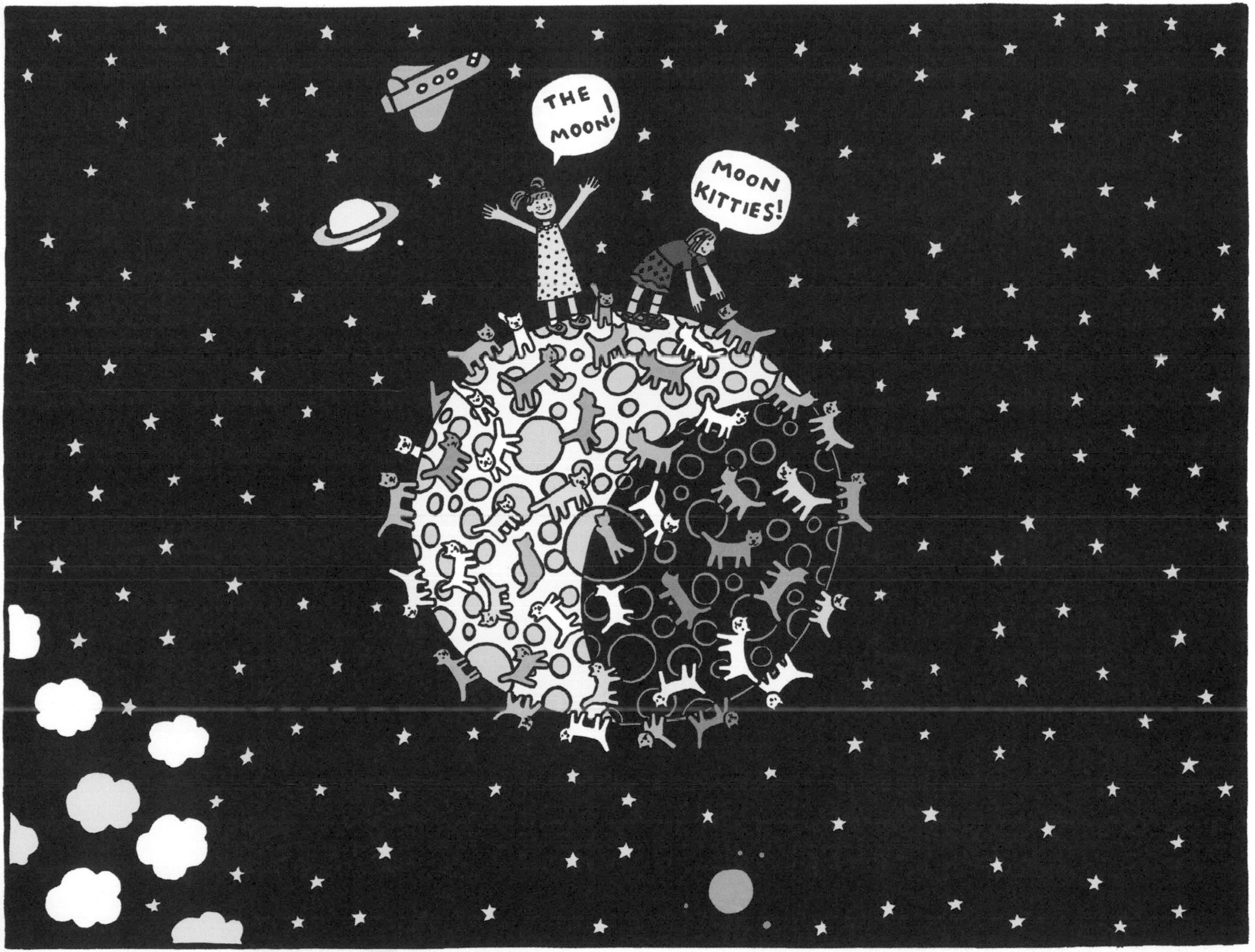
THE MOON!
MOON KITTIES!

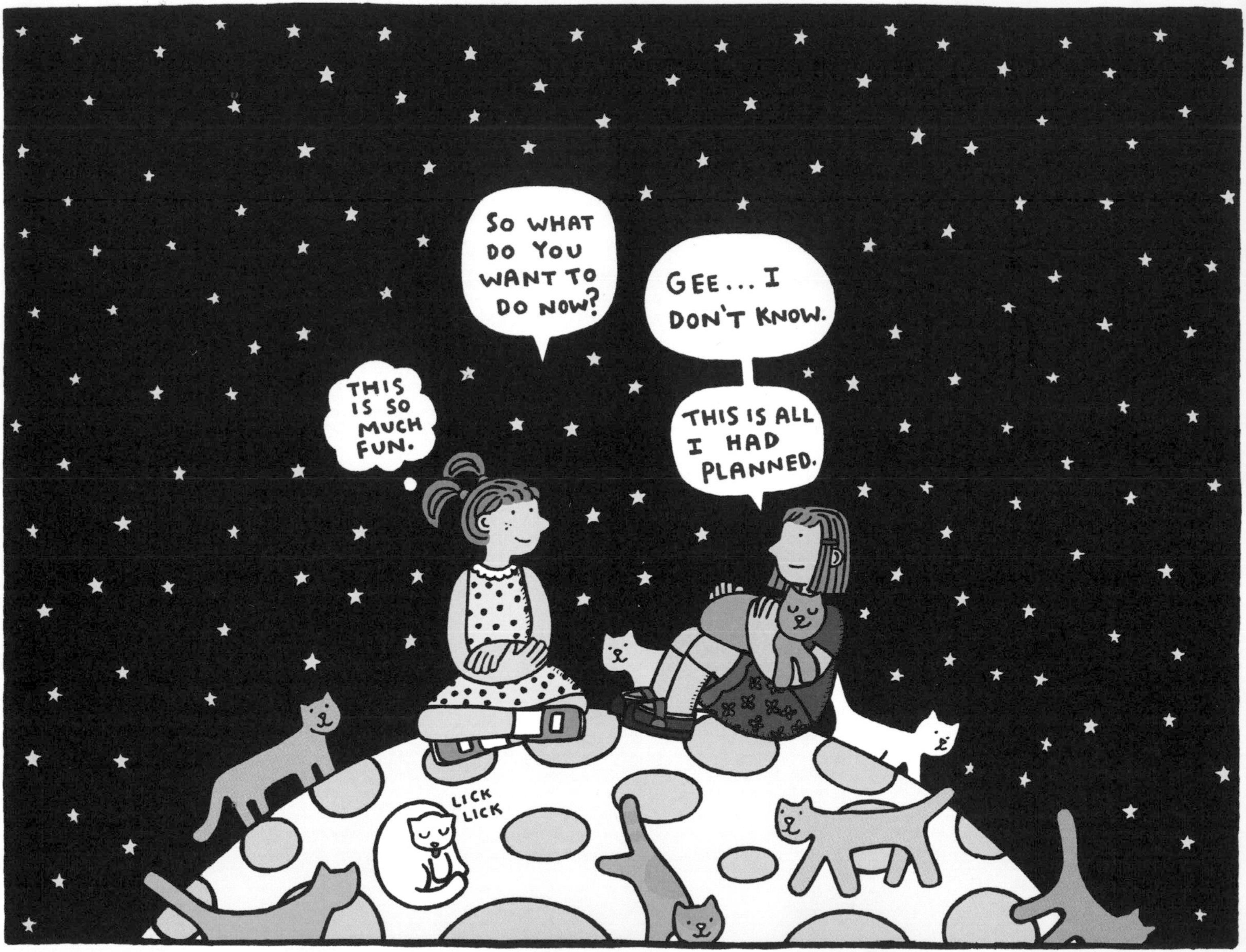
THIS IS SO MUCH FUN.
SO WHAT DO YOU WANT TO DO NOW?
GEE... I DON'T KNOW.
THIS IS ALL I HAD PLANNED.
LICK LICK

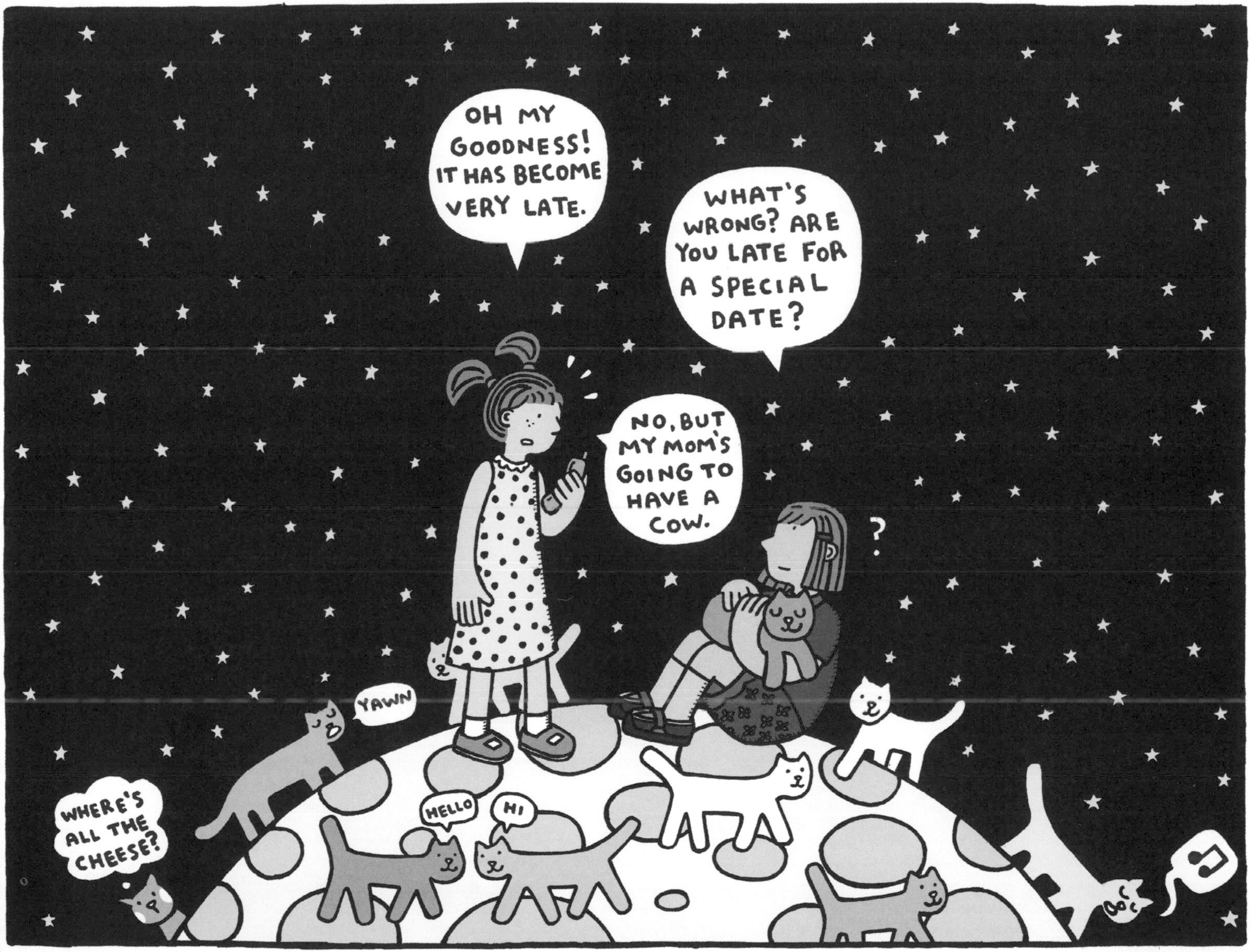
OH MY GOODNESS! IT HAS BECOME VERY LATE.
WHAT'S WRONG? ARE YOU LATE FOR A SPECIAL DATE?
NO, BUT MY MOM'S GOING TO HAVE A COW.
?
YAWN
WHERE'S ALL THE CHEESE?
HELLO
HI

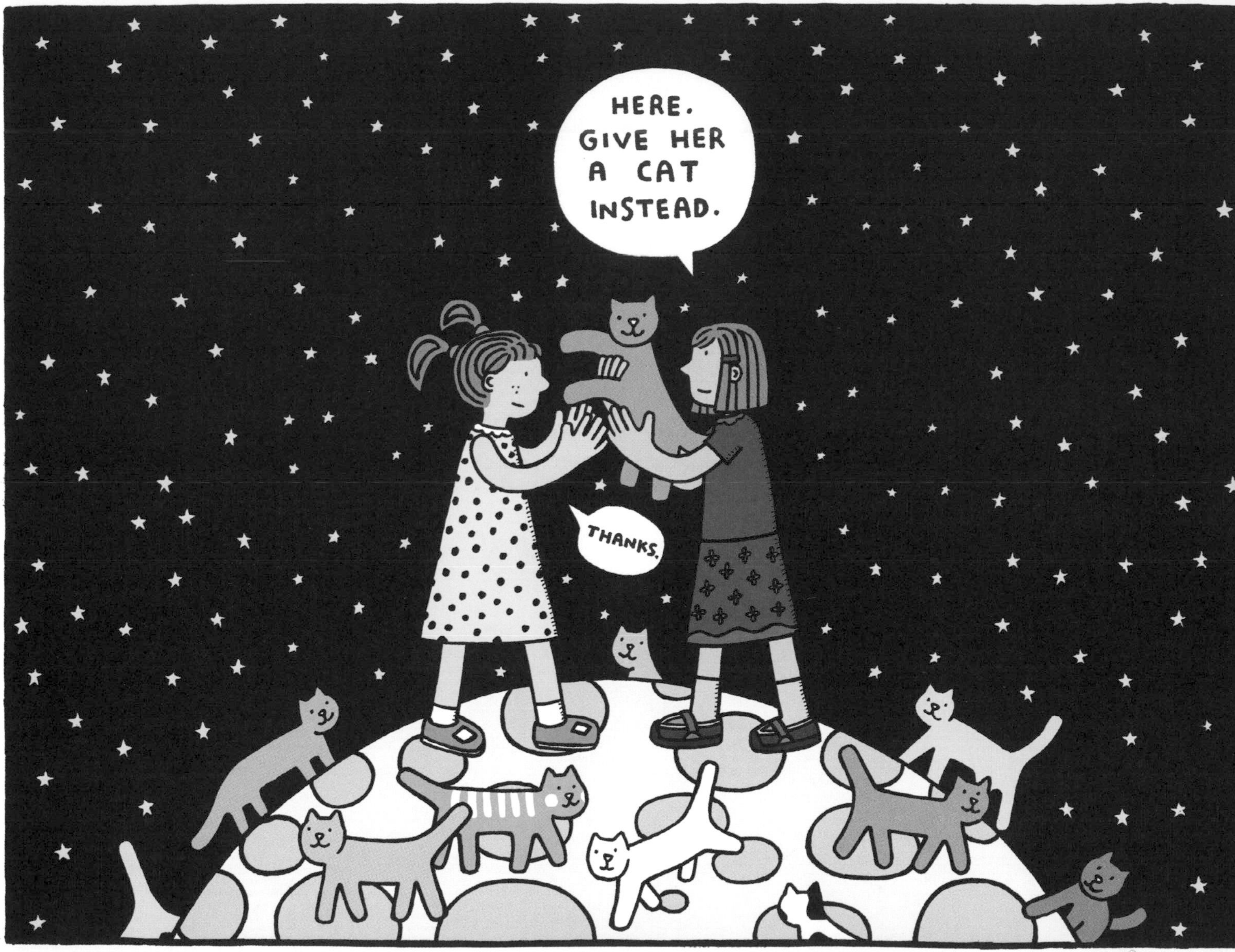
HERE. GIVE HER A CAT INSTEAD.
THANKS.

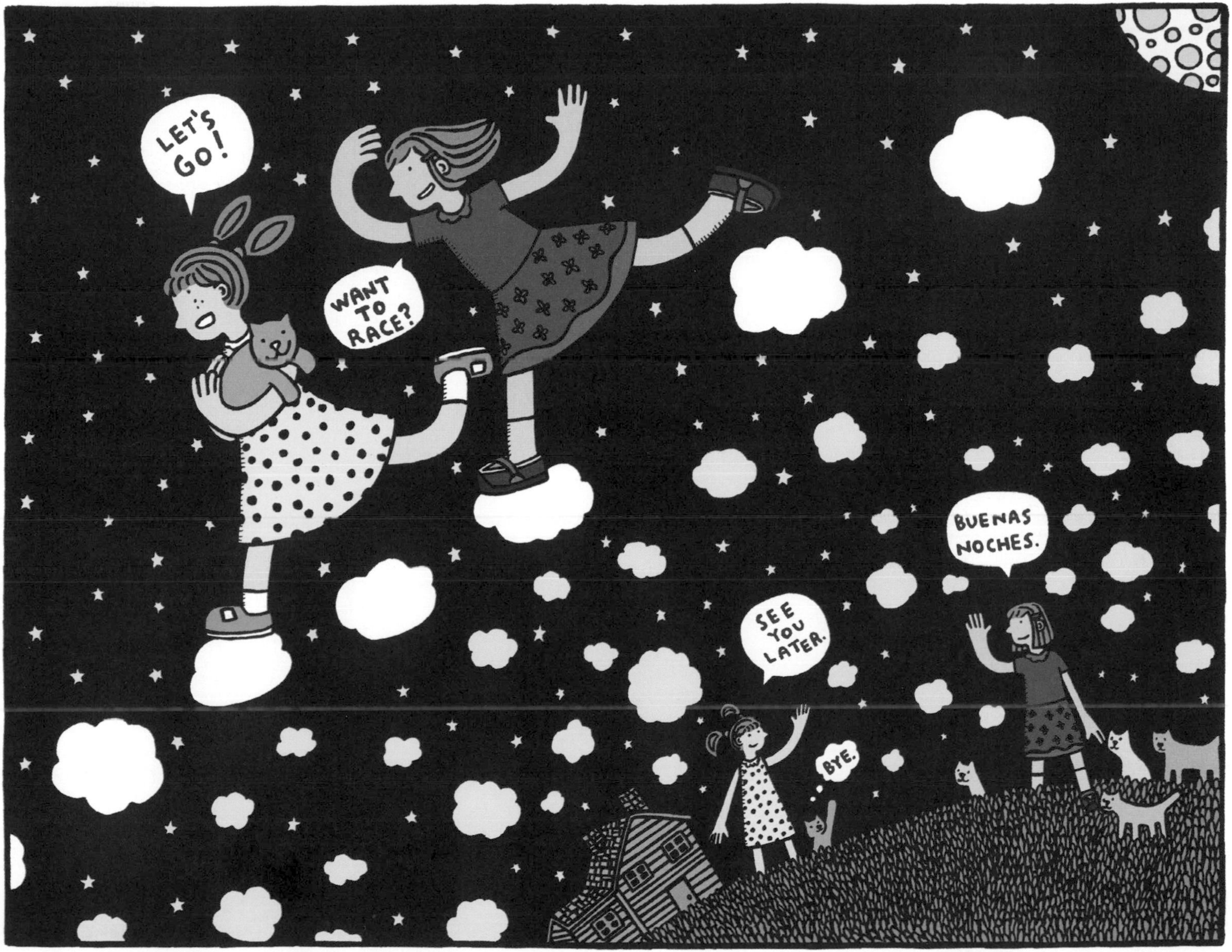
LET'S GO!
WANT TO RACE?
SEE YOU LATER.
BUENAS NOCHES.
BYE.

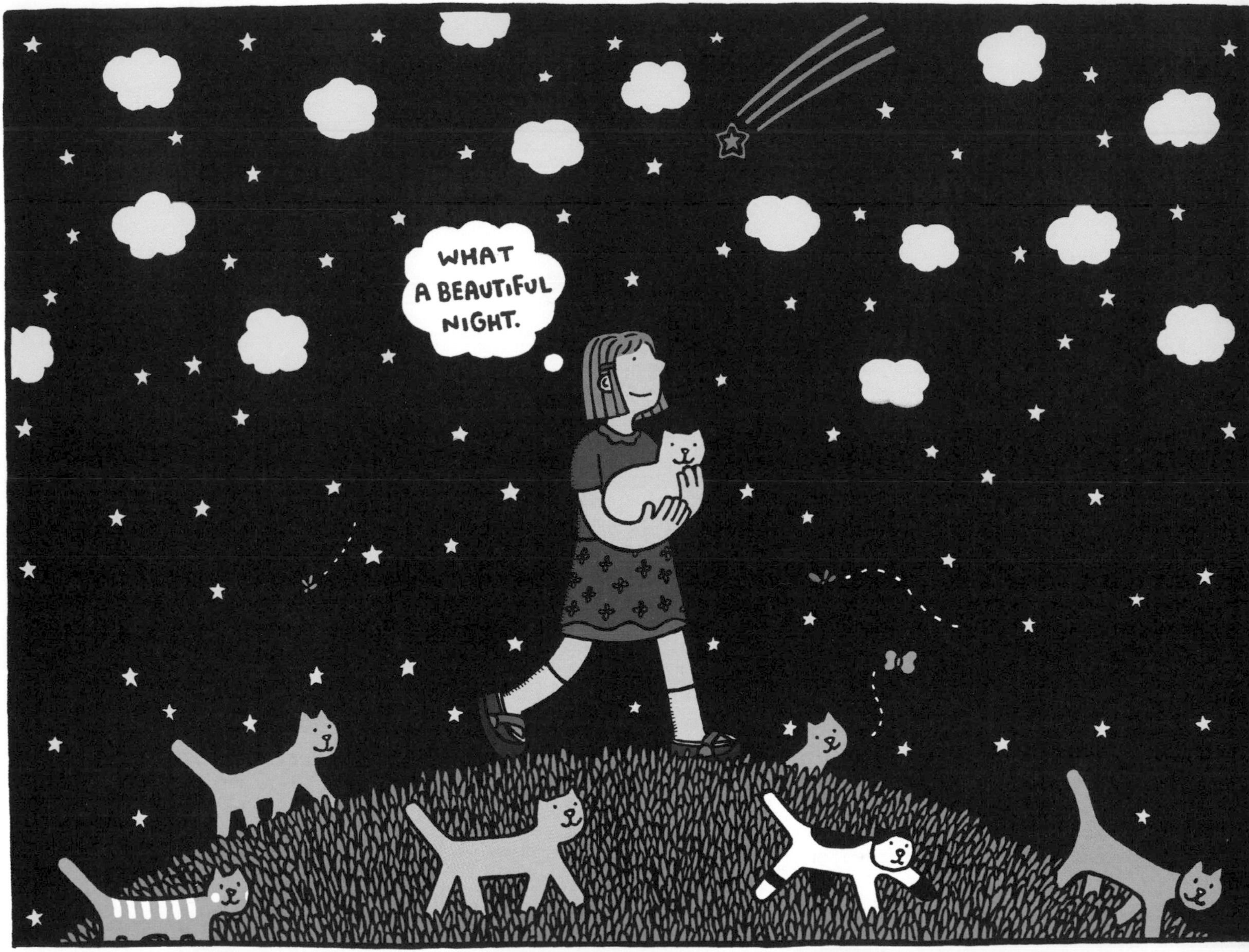
WHAT A BEAUTIFUL NIGHT.

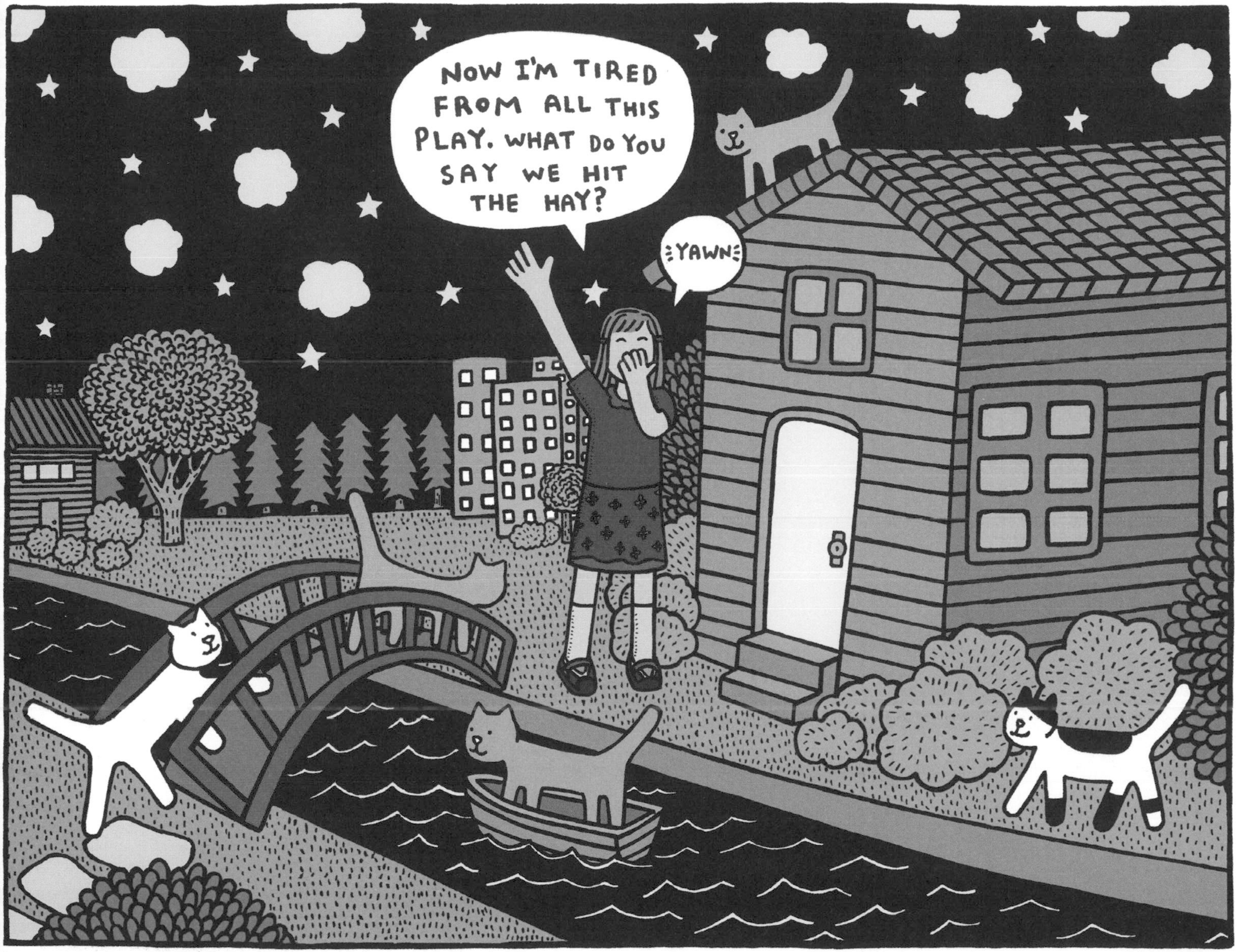
NOW I'M TIRED FROM ALL THIS PLAY. WHAT DO YOU SAY WE HIT THE HAY?
YAWN

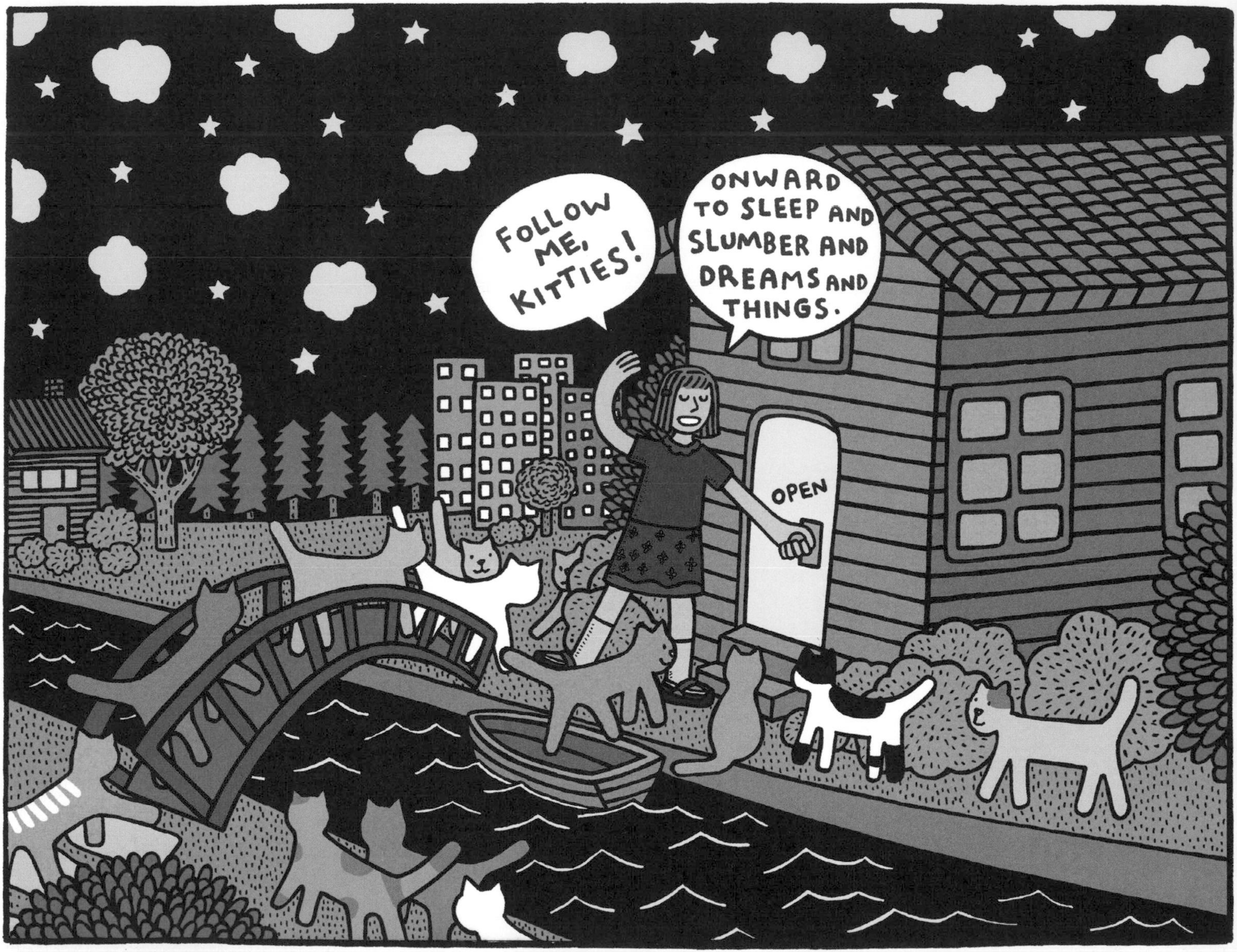
FOLLOW ME, KITTIES!
ONWARD TO SLEEP AND SLUMBER AND DREAMS AND THINGS.
OPEN

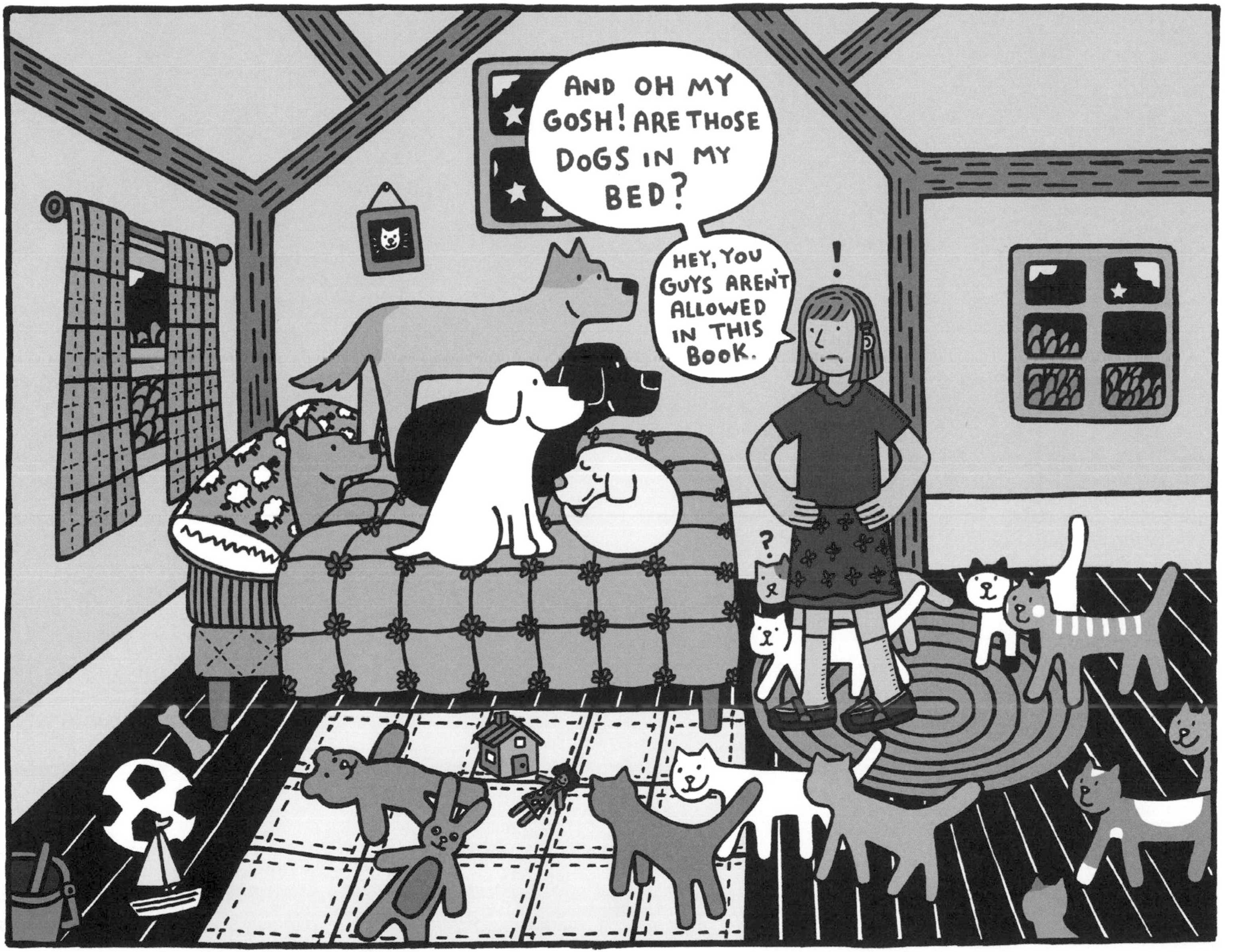
AND OH MY GOSH! ARE THOSE DOGS IN MY BED?
HEY, YOU GUYS AREN'T ALLOWED IN THIS BOOK.
!
?

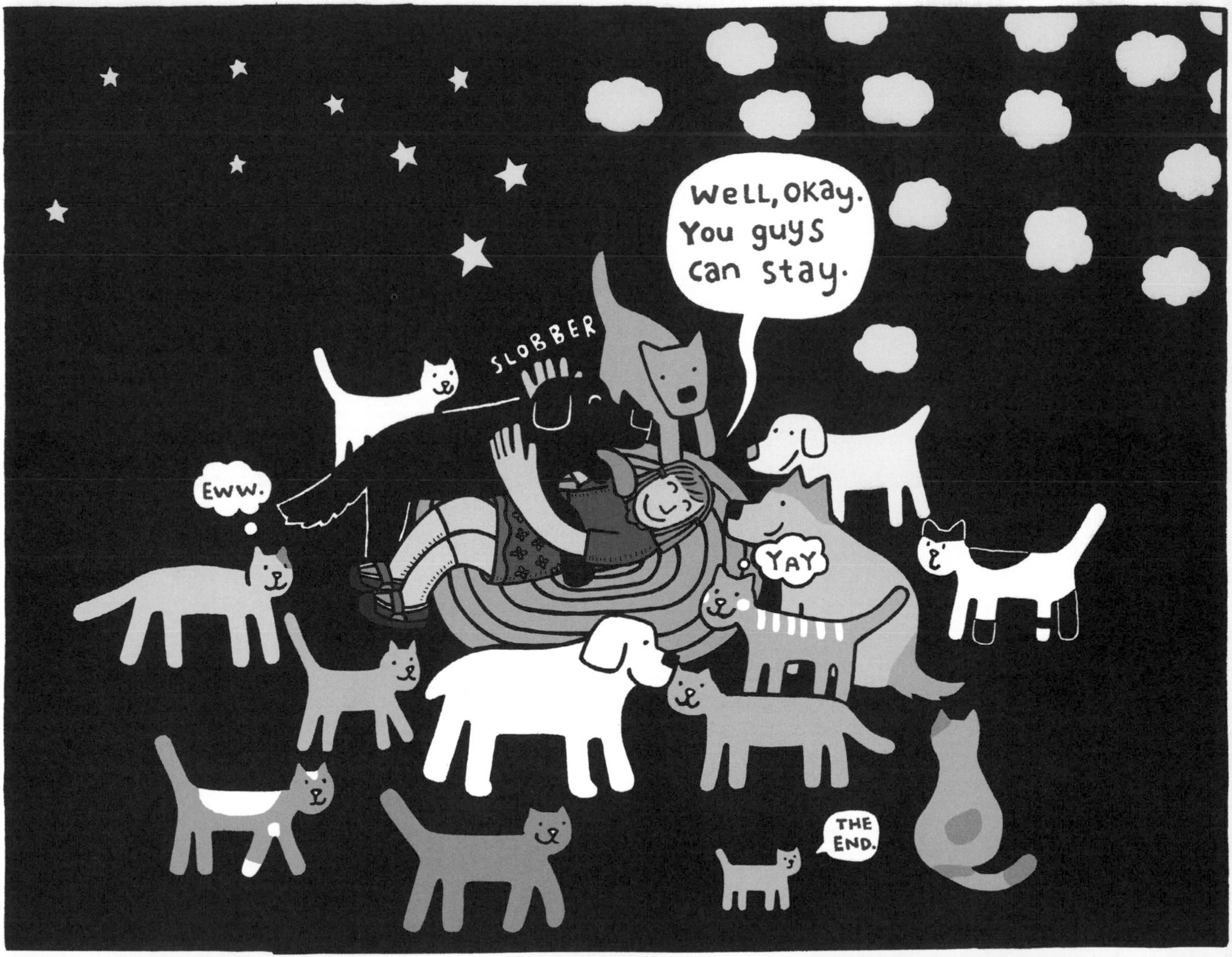
Well, okay. You guys can stay.
SLOBBER
EWW.
YAY
THE END.

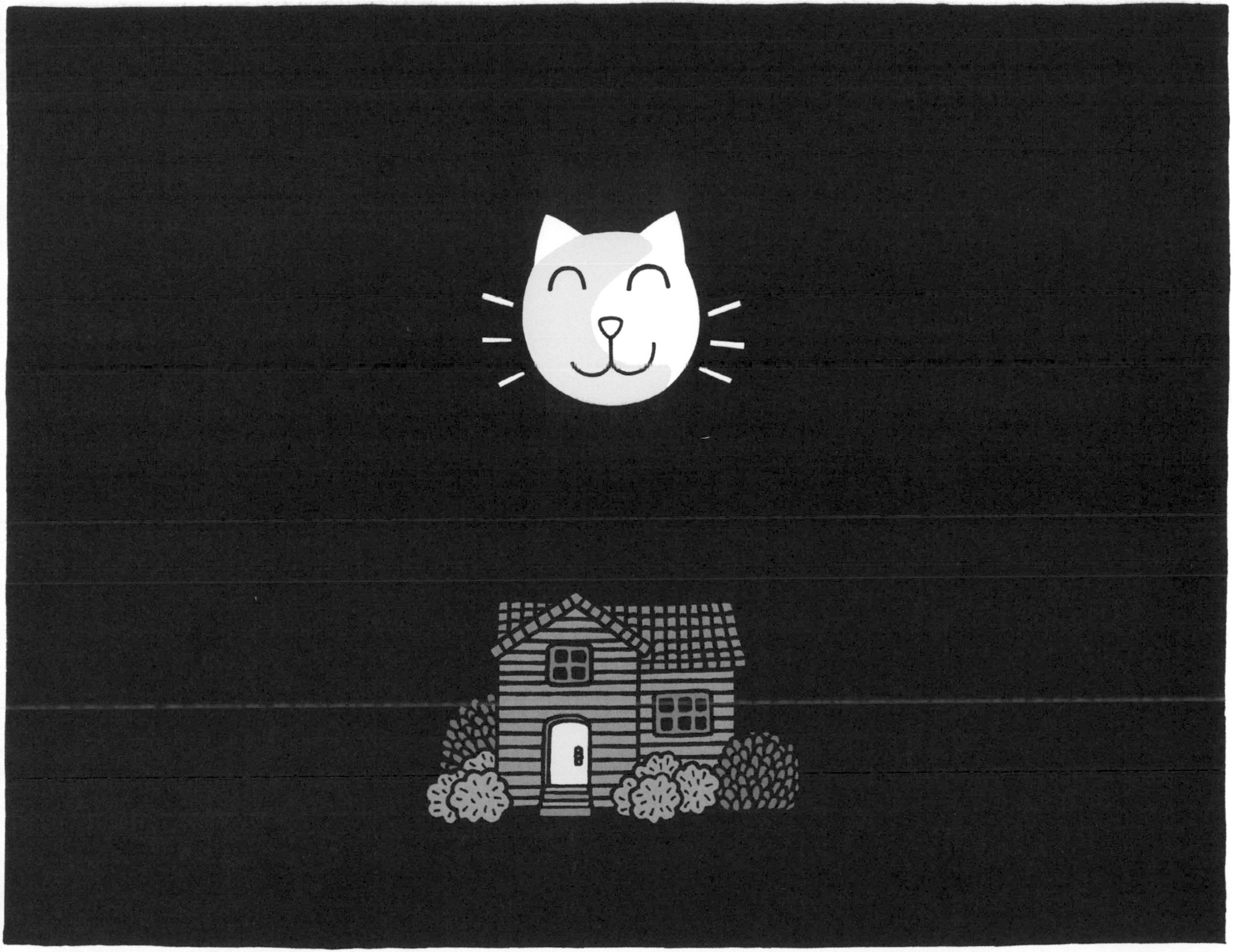